OTHER PEOPLE WE MARRIED

STORIES

EMMA STRAUB

FIVECHAPTERS
BOOKS

www.fivechapters.com
www.emmastraub.net

"Some People Must Really Fall in Love" appeared in The Saint Ann's Review.
"Rosemary" appeared in Cousin Corinne's Reminder.
"Pearls" appeared on The Nervous Breakdown.
"Abraham's Enchanted Forest" appeared in Juked.
"Puttanesca" appeared on FiveChapters.
"Fly-Over State" and "Hot Springs Eternal" were published by FlatmanCrooked
Publishing, both in their fiction anthologies
and as a stand-alone book.

Library of Congress Cataloging-in-Publication Data
Straub, Emma
Other People We Married: Stories / by Emma Straub.—1st ed.
p.   cm.
ISBN: 978-0-982-93921-5
Library of Congress Control Number: 2010938976

Book interior design by Michael Fusco

Manufactured in the United States of America
Published February 2011
First Printing

For my parents, Clint Eastwood and Miss America,
with love and gratitude.

CONTENTS

SOME PEOPLE MUST REALLY
FALL IN LOVE

In the living room, the conversation was about teacher/
student romance. Most of the party-goers were clustered
in the dining room, standing around the table snacking on
brie and carrot sticks, but a small contingent from the English
department sat on comfortable chairs, enjoying the elbow
room.

"It's funny, though, isn't it?" Karen Bernstein taught a class
on Modernism. "It used to be sort of cliché, this idea of the
lecherous guy, but now it's all twenty-five-year-old blonde
women! They just can't keep their hands off!" She grabbed the
air.

"Right, right—like that woman who had babies with an
eleven-year-old—what was her name?" Julie Specter taught
Victorian lit, big novels with lots of characters. She was terrible
with names.

"Mary Lou? Mary Beth? Something like that." Laura
Reagan was the youngest professor in the department, and
watched the most television. She looked at me, the second
youngest, for confirmation.

"Mary Kay?" I said, trying to sound tentative. Everyone repeated it.

"But what do you think it's all about? Karen asked. "Really, I mean, why would a grown woman be interested in a teenage boy?"

Julie had two sons, ages twelve and fourteen. "They wouldn't if they knew how bad their socks smelled," she said.

One of the poets was hovering in the open doorway, a plastic glass of red wine in her hand, filled all the way to the top. She was new.

"I think it's because they still think they're sixteen," Laura said. "They're under-developed. You know, stunted." She opened her eyes wide. The poet in the doorway took a big gulp of wine and wandered back towards the food. I wished I could follow, but I was sure that if I left the room just then, everyone would know. They would notice that I was wearing eyeliner for the first time in five years. I stayed put and said "Uh-huh" at appropriate intervals.

Three of us shared a small office. Our desks were all pushed against the walls, so that when we were all in at the same time, the backs of our chairs were nearly touching. Laura sat in the middle, I sat closer to the door, and Jeff Lansky faced the opposite wall. We taught whatever they told us to, which meant the beginner classes: how to read, how to write, how to argue your case. I walked in with my lunch in a paper bag and Laura and Jeff were huddled together, giggling.

"What's up?" I sat down and my chair wheezed.

Laura got up and peeked out into the hallway, her little

bird hands clutching either side of the doorframe. As far as I knew, she only ate vanilla yogurt and saltines.

"Well," she said, looking back to Jeff. "This student of mine just came in, you know, for a conference…" She covered her mouth with her hand. Laura was pretty and wore office-appropriate attire, including heels. She had make-up on every day, foundation and everything.

"Go on," Jeff said, winking at her. Jeff was the only gay guy in the whole department, and sometimes I felt sorry for him, that all he had was us.

"And I've never been so positive in my entire life that someone had a crush on me." She opened her mouth, wide, in mock disbelief, the kind of look eager moms get when trick-or-treaters ring the doorbell on Halloween. "It was so cute! He said, 'Miss Reagan, my band is playing at the Union this weekend, and it would be so cool if you came.' He blushed! I always thought he was sort of tough, you know, like a bad boy!"

"Plus you saw him checking out your boobs." Jeff winked at me. He loved to wink.

"Plus I saw him checking out my boobs!" Laura did not usually use the word 'boobs,' or any other less-than-clinical term to describe her own anatomy. Reddish streaks appeared in her cleavage, as though her boobs themselves couldn't quite believe the attention they'd received.

"He totally has a crush on you," Jeff said, crossing his legs and leaning towards Laura's desk. "It was really cute."

"Sorry I missed it." I pulled my lunch out of the bag, and lined up all the items on my desk: tuna-fish sandwich. Lemon-flavored iced tea. Chocolate-chip cookie. "Do all your students really call you 'Miss Reagan?'" I asked.

She puffed out her lips and tapped her finger against them. "Yeah, I guess so. Why, what do yours call you, Amy?"

"Mostly they don't call me anything, unless they need something. They just point, usually," I said, twisting the bottle of iced tea on the desk. It made a chalky sound, and Jeff and Laura both stood up to put on their jackets.

"Sorry, guys, didn't mean to drive you out." I took a bite of my sandwich. They both waved.

I wondered when Jeff had last had sex, if that sort of thing was hard to come by in a town so small. Maybe he met people at the gym. He was always talking about going to the gym. When Jeff had first moved out from the East Coast, he'd been slender, like a dancer. He'd always had a really lovely, long neck. Now his neck just seemed like another part of his body. He was starting to look more like the locals, and more like we could have been related. After they were gone, I ate my lunch and then brushed my teeth in the bathroom.

On Thursdays, I taught my beginning creative-writing course. I had twenty-five freshmen, most of who were disinclined to believe me when I said that poetry didn't have to rhyme and that stories didn't have to have morals at the end. We sat around several large tables that had been pushed together sometime in the early 1980s, some years before my students were born. The room had no windows and smelled vaguely of body odor; it got worse in the spring when the layers began to come off, like my students were twenty-five little onions, all waiting patiently to make me cry.

Paul sat on the other end of the table, directly across from me. There were other kids on his right and other kids on his left but Paul was in the middle. Sometimes I closed my eyes and pretended that the other students vanished into thin air, not forever, but just for a few minutes, long enough for me to walk around the table and get a closer look without any distractions. The blackboard was on his side of the room and I liked to use it to write out announcements that I just as easily could have sent in an email. If I was on that side of the room, I could look down at the part of his blond hair and the straight line of his nose. His side of the room never smelled like feet or farts or armpits. He smelled like cheap shampoo. I imagined his walking down the aisles of a drugstore, unscrewing bottles to sniff their contents. He would close his eyes, and picture fields of lavender, buckets of April rain, orange groves.

"Who knows what onomatopoeia means?" I asked the class, scratching the chalk against the blackboard.

They sat in stunned silence, staring at the blank pages of their notebooks as if hoping to find the answer written there. Paul looked at me over his shoulder, pale eyebrows raised. I guessed that he was eighteen, nineteen at the most. Some nights I lay awake thinking, You know, he could have taken a few years off after high school; he could be twenty. That would only put seven years between us, seven wasn't much. But he wasn't twenty. He was a teenager. Things that happen in seven years: Brad Pitt in Tibet. The itch.

"Buzz," I said, looking at Paul and smiling. "Whirr. Fizz. Glug." He turned back around and dutifully copied down the spelling.

I used a red pen to mark the students' work. Mostly they wrote about being in college, or their hometowns, which were usually towns in either Ohio or Pennsylvania with a few stoplights and no hope for the future. Some of them enjoyed reading; these were the troublemakers. They'd stop using punctuation and stop making sense and think that they were Kerouac, or, worse yet, Faulkner. Sometimes I would use a smiley face to let them know I was still being encouraging. I put polite check marks in random places on the rest of the pages and stuck them together with a paperclip.

Rebecca sat next to Paul and was my enemy. She turned in handwritten poems about broken hearts, grade-school mush. If Laura or Jeff had been her teacher, she might have come around. She wanted assignments; she wanted to be told what to do. Laura loved a project. One student of hers had recently been released from prison and had trouble with grammar. Laura met with him every day for two hours, even over the summer. She told me that it was the best thing that ever happened to her, after meeting her fiancé, Brian. Brian was in the law school and was big enough to kick the shit out of anyone, prison or no. I think that made her feel more comfortable about the situation.

The rules were cloudy on purpose; the instructor explained that while it was not against the law for us to have relationships with our students, it was frowned upon. During our day-long diversity training, we were told a story about a professor who had dated one of his students, only to have the affair end messily halfway through the semester. It wasn't about the law, the diversity specialist said. The question was about grading, and fairness to the other students. We all sat on folding chairs in a room in the student union, trying not to fall asleep, or to run screaming from the room. We were teachers; of course we had excellent morals. At the time, I hadn't met Paul. I didn't know they made teenaged boys that looked like him, like actors whose private lives you'd read about on the Internet. Someone had seen a boy like him, though. That's why the rules were the way they were; it had to be. Some people must have really fallen in love.

Karen the modernist had a friend from yoga class; she wanted us to meet. I didn't know what kind of guy did yoga, or what kind of woman he'd want to meet. I couldn't wrap my legs around my head, if that's what he was expecting. Laura wrote my number down and handed it to Karen, agreeing for me. Jeff winked. "Blind dates are sexy," he said.

I met Martin at the restaurant. Karen and Laura had been raving about it for months. "Finally, a real place to eat," they said. "It's just like being in New York." The food was supposed to be small and expensive, hard to eat.

Martin was standing outside waiting. He was taller than me, which I liked, and slim, which I'd anticipated, given his bendy origins. He was wearing khaki pants and a black sweater; he'd dressed up. I still had on what I'd been wearing all day: blue jeans and a cardigan that hung baggily from my shoulders. I watched Martin wonder if I was me.

"Hi," I said, approaching. My clogs clunked to a halt. "I'm Amy."

Martin smiled nervously, revealing two even rows of very small teeth. "Shall we?" He pointed towards the thick glass door. Inside, large groups of well-heeled undergraduates gestured with their chopsticks.

"Great!" I said, stupidly, and let him open the door.

They sat us at a table against the wall, which meant that I faced the room, while Martin faced only me. The room smelled like pheromones and soy sauce. I was suddenly famished.

"So," Martin began, trying to catch my eye. "Karen says you teach in the English department?"

"Yes." She'd told me that he was an engineer, or a computer programmer, and divorced. His hair was thin and feathery on top. "And you do yoga?"

Martin bowed in what I perceived to be a very yogic manner, and bared his small teeth again. A waiter appeared next to us, a kid with a beaded necklace and a surfer's tan. I hated for him to find out we were in Ohio; how painful that would be. I wanted him to say "Aloha," but instead he just asked if we wanted anything to drink.

"Yes, please," I said, turning towards Martin. "Don't you think we'd better?"

The surfer brought back two small carafes of something that smelled and tasted vaguely of rubbing alcohol. I drank mine quickly and ordered another.

"So, go on blind dates a lot?" The sake was making Martin's teeth look more human-sized. "What do you like to read? Have you ever written any poetry? How long have you lived in Ohio?"

He cleared his throat. I wondered what his ex-wife looked

like, if she was a brunette like me, if I was his type, if people still talked about their 'types.' Martin looked forty, maybe late-thirties, which made him approximately thirteen years older than me. Thirteen was almost two times seven. He opened the menu.

"I'm a vegetarian," he said. "Ooh, they have edamame." He looked at me over the metallic sheen of the menu. "I went to a place just like this in Japan once."

Behind him, the room was filling. Girls wore high heels and short dresses too slight for the still-cool weather outside. They opened their mouths and laughed, on dates with each other. They weren't interested in freshman boys; they needed football players, or older guys. I thought about offering up Martin—he had a house, a car. They could do yoga together.

"Order whatever you want, I'll eat anything," I said. "I'll be right back."

I followed a clump of girls into the women's bathroom. There were four of them all dressed nearly identically. It was like one of the picture puzzles in the back pages of old comic books—which of these is different? I drew imaginary circles around one girl's tiny skirt, another's cowboy boots. The bathroom was small and dark, with wooden panels on the wall. The girls clattered together towards the mirror. I ducked behind them into one of the empty stalls. Girls that pretty didn't have bladders, it turned out. Another point for evolution! I made a note to remember to bring that up with Martin—engineers knew about science, I'm sure he'd be interested. Another mental note—make sure he's an engineer.

"Oh my God, Jessie, did you see that guy? The waiter? With

the necklace? I wanted to lick him." It was Cowboy Boots.

"I know! Me too! We should order lots more drinks and then leave him our phone number on the check. Oh my God. We totally should." Tiny Skirt was agreeing with herself.

Maybe I could write my phone number on the bottom of one of Paul's poems: *If you ever want to talk about your work outside of class, just give me a call. I'm not in the office much, so this is the best way to reach me.* I could pretend not to have an email address, or a campus mailbox. I could convince Laura and Jeff to make my desk look abandoned.

The girls clucked and clattered out in formation. The room was filled with the echo of their energy. I peed, and noticed that there was music playing. The song was about love, love, love, crazy love.

It was midterms and we all had streams of students coming in, further crowding the small office with heaps of coats and backpacks. Jeff talked loudly and recommended books that I knew he hadn't actually read. He talked in a booming voice, all confidence, all machismo. His students loved him. Sometimes they'd dawdle outside the door, just hoping he'd show up. They'd lean against the walls with all different parts of their bodies: upper backs, legs, faces. They'd twist themselves into pretzels, just for him. He had the answers, they just knew it. He'd know how their story should end, what they should write their essay about, what made a good poem great. Really he just repeated whatever they'd said, phrasing it in a more emphatic way. No one ever noticed. It was brilliant.

Rebecca was my twelve-thirty. She peeked in the open

door and looked almost disappointed to find me sitting exactly where I was supposed to be. She had a face like a sewer rat—pointed and sniveling, her nose out of in front of everything else. It wiggled.

"So," I said, once she was sitting in the chair next to my desk, "how are things?"

"Fine, I guess." She wrinkled her rat-nose.

Behind me, Laura was having a discussion with a student who'd read a Henry James novel. "Mm hmm," she said. "Long sentences."

Rebecca opened her notebook and waited for me to speak.

"You know what?" I said. "You're fine. We really don't have that much to talk about. I just wanted to check in." I smiled at her like I meant it. She stared at my left clog as it dangled off my toes and threatened to drop.

"Okay," she said, her voice as reedy as her face, all pinched. I wondered what her parents were like, if they genuinely liked her or just loved her like they were supposed to. "I was just wondering, you know, about my grade." The good ones wondered about their writing. The bad ones wondered about their grade. This was an easy distinction. Sometimes I thought about lowering students' grades every time they brought it up.

"I wouldn't worry about it," I said. "Just make sure you type all the assignments, and that you've turned everything in. You should be fine." This was true. Rebecca scooped up her book bag and was out the door before I could say anything else. The entire conference had lasted three minutes. I shuffled through my papers and listened to Jeff talk about the passive voice. Laura explained the difference between lay and lie.

In between students, Laura showed us pictures from her sister's wedding on Long Island. She was the maid-of-honor and wore Vera Wang. The ceremony was on the beach—it was beautiful. Everyone cried, even the priest.

"So, Amy, how was the date?" It had taken Laura two long days to ask.

"It was fine, I suppose." I thought about Martin's thin arms. They seemed sad in retrospect—toned for what? For who? "He was a nice guy, but, you know…" I said. Trailing off seemed polite, as though I was conflicted.

Laura looked concerned. She clasped her bony hands in front of her bony chest. "But what? Are you going to see him again?" Her voice was higher than usual. Brian was Laura's second fiancé. She'd kept the first ring, and sometimes wore it on her other hand. It was sitting there now, looking at me sideways. It told me that I wasn't getting any younger and that it was really time to stop wasting valuable opportunities.

Paul was early. His backpack was enormous and made him look like a long, lanky turtle—the kind of turtle who probably ran cross-country in high school. Somehow his hair seemed lighter than usual, as though he'd found all the sunlight in Ohio.

"Hey," he said, addressing me.

"Hey," I said, wishing I'd thought to buy a lint roller, ever.

Laura and Jeff squeaked their chairs closer together. I couldn't decide whether I wished they were paying more or less attention.

"So," Paul said, sinking down to the chair. He ran his hands over the metal arms.

"So," I said. He was a turtle, and I was a parrot. "Paul."

He smoothed out his corduroys. They were the color of Bahamian sand and loose around his legs. His eyes were the color of cold water—a pond. His hair was the color of straw. My brain had turned into one of Rebecca's poems. It was still my turn to speak.

"Your story was good," I said. "Really impressive."

He blushed, and turned his face to the side. "Thanks. Really? Thanks. That's really nice."

I could feel myself blushing back. "Well," I said, "it's easy to be nice when something's actually good." Who was talking? I could hear Laura's head turn towards me, away from her sister's wedding, away from Jeff's open mouth. Up close it was easier to remember that Paul was young, too young, but it was also easier to see how well-proportioned his features were. He had shoulders like a swimmer, and a long back. He reminded me of the boy I'd lost my virginity to, at an embarrassingly late age. He had been too handsome for me, like Paul was too handsome for me, but age seemed to smooth that out. He wanted me to like him. He was trying to make me like him.

One day, I asked Jeff where he went to meet people—not people like me, but people who he might want to see with their clothes off. The Rooster was on the outskirts of town—a mile down the four-lane road that led to the airport. A couple of normal-looking Ohio guys—Carhartt jackets, boots—stood outside and smoked. A small decal of a rainbow stuck to the window, well below eye level.

I followed Jeff in through the blacked-out door. The bar was long and dark and my eyes had to adjust. I half-expected to see guys performing sex acts in every booth, but instead it looked just like any other bar—mostly guys, mostly sitting alone. Jeff nodded at the bartender, but I couldn't tell if the nod was meant to communicate anything other than hello. He led us towards two stools at the end of the bar. An out-of-date calendar hung on the wall in front of us, welcoming us to 2004. In 2004, Paul would have been fifteen, still a boy. He would have slept in a twin-sized bed, eaten breakfast prepared by his mother. I wondered how tall he was then, if his feet hung off the couch when he watched television. Some boys grew late.

"Want a drink?" Jeff looked amused. He seemed more handsome inside the bar, more relaxed. It was as though there, everyone knew, and there was no pretense, no need for an awkward explanation.

"Sure," I said. "Vodka tonic?"

"Two vodka tonics," he said in the direction of the bartender.

"So," I said, swiveling my seat left and right, left and right. "Come here often?"

Jeff laughed. "Actually, yes."

It occurred to me suddenly that Jeff might be an alcoholic in addition to a homosexual and maybe I should back off. "That's cool," I said. "That's cool."

"So, Laura told me that you have the major hots for one of your students." Jeff winked.

"No," I said. "Well, maybe." I tried to take a long slug of

my drink and stabbed myself in the cheek with the thin plastic straw. "That's really bad to admit, isn't it?"

Jeff shrugged. "Not really. It used to happen to me all the time."

"Students?" I asked. There was so much more to Jeff. Maybe he and I could talk about Laura, like he and Laura talked about everyone else. Maybe together we could get her to eat something, and then she would thank us forever.

"No, but straight guys. In middle school, high school, that sort of thing. I always had crushes on the straight guys. Sometimes it's nice to have something you know you can't do anything about. Sort of Jedi, you know?"

"Jedi?" Behind us, someone played Dolly Parton on the jukebox. Gay bars were so much better than straight bars. It was like a secret world where no one was embarrassed about anything.

"Like a Jedi mind trick—you know, all self-discipline." Jeff was thirty-three. Every year we had a birthday lunch for him in the office. I wondered if he came here afterwards, to really celebrate. I wonder what kind of presents people gave him, whether they were better than the coasters I'd given him. He went on. "It's like a built-in understanding that you are going to be disappointed, and being okay with that."

"But what if it could actually work? There have to be exceptions, right? Some people must really fall in love," I said, thinking about something I'd read about Dolly Parton's husband and how he's never seen her without make-up and how she has to go to award shows by herself because he doesn't like the spotlight. That was weird, but it worked for them.

"Well," Jeff said. "There was the one guy in ninth grade who let me jerk him off in the broom closet."

That made us both chuckle into our drinks for a minute. The bar was getting more crowded; it was time to go. "So, Jeff, why don't you have a boyfriend?"

He smiled. "I do have a boyfriend. David Bernard, history."

"With the… from the seventh floor?!" David Bernard was shorter than I was and completely bald. His head gleamed. "Why didn't you ever tell me?"

Jeff stood up and dropped a few bills onto the bar. "Because, Amy, you never asked." He was still smiling as he led me out the way we'd come in.

Martin didn't sound as surprised to hear from me as I thought he would—he was used to the protocol. We agreed to meet at his house for dinner. Martin lived on the other side of town, where most of the professors lived. His house was on one of the nicer streets, one that faced a nature preserve and a lake that rented paddleboats in the summer. Laura and Brian were looking at a condo nearby. I slowed down and checked the mailboxes for his number.

Both the inside and outside lights were on, so I could see the house clearly. Martin was considerate that way. A dog barked somewhere nearby—a small dog. A flagstone path led up to the door. I could hear some jazz playing inside, and I waited for a minute before ringing the bell. I'd shaved my legs and worn a skirt.

Martin opened the door promptly. He had an apron tied around his narrow waist, and he patted his hands dry on it before pulling me close for a kiss on the cheek. He hadn't been divorced long.

The living room was dominated by tasteful objects—pieces of art from other countries, lots of rugs. It was the house where a grown-up lived. He brought me a glass of white wine—dinner was almost ready. We ate sitting on pillows beside a low table. Martin had spent a few weeks in Japan a decade ago. It was where he'd met his wife—on the same tour of a temple outside Tokyo. Some things just stuck, he said.

When his clothes were off, Martin's body looked exactly the way I expected, but with all the unforeseeable eccentricities of a human body—a freckle here, a birthmark, tufts of colorful hair. We didn't talk about whether or not it was a good idea, or whether or not I was on birth control. We weren't drunk. It was just two people doing something that people do. I thought about Jeff and a straight boy hiding in a broom closet. Just because something was impossible didn't mean it couldn't happen. I thought about Paul's shoulders and nose and my bare skin prickled. Maybe Martin wouldn't mind growing his hair out a little on the sides; maybe if it was longer it would look a little thicker. Maybe Martin had his own paddleboat and could use the lake whenever he wanted—maybe he could teach me some words in Japanese and the best way to use friction in various circumstances. When it was over, I went home.

Laura took me to the mall—now that I was seeing someone, it was time for a new look, she said. She'd seen a show on cable where these two good-looking fashion experts threw away everything in a woman's closet and then made her buy what they told her to. She said it was just what I needed, plus some new underwear. New underwear was important.

"Do you have any thongs?" Laura asked. "Boy shorts?"

"Are you speaking English?" The walls were pink—it was like being inside a gumball machine. The sexy stuff was in the back, Laura said, pulling my arm.

I saw Paul before I heard him—he was walking down the main aisle of the mall with two other boys, boys just like him, only less advanced. I shoved the small pile of underwear into Laura's hands and rushed outside, ducking slightly behind a large potted plant. The three boys vanished into a clothing store that looked like a nightclub—a dark-paneled fake porch swallowed them. Posters of larger-than-life disembodied torsos flexed and shone like diamonds, beveled to the point of unassailable perfection.

Laura appeared beside me, clutching a plastic shopping bag. "What the hell?" she said. "Panties are your friend."

"Shush!" I clamped my hand over her mouth and pulled her down next to me. Our knees rested uncomfortably against the large ceramic pot. The green stalks growing out of it were plastic.

Paul and his friends reemerged. He was chewing gum, and wearing shorts. This is what he would be like, I thought, if we never had anywhere to be, if we were always on vacation. I didn't care what Laura thought. I wasn't even in the mall anymore, I was somewhere else. I was in my forties, in my fifties. I was in the grocery store and bumping into Paul. We were exchanging phone numbers, two grown-ups. It happened all the time.

ROSEMARY

Claire didn't want to tell her husband that she'd called a pet psychic. Matt was a lawyer and scoffed easily. She told him that Vivian was a friend from her post-natal yoga class, and wasn't he always saying she should have more friends? Matt was glad that the cat was gone, Claire could tell. He'd helped her put up the flyers in the neighborhood: up one street and down the next, but his heart wasn't in it. Rosemary was not an easy cat to love, but that was no excuse. As Claire sometimes liked to say, she'd been sleeping with Rosemary ten years longer than she's been sleeping with Matt, so it was just something he was going to have to deal with. It was a permanent relationship. Claire expected tears.

Rosemary had been missing for four days before Claire found Vivian's name on a flyer at the yoga studio on Court Street.

"Are you full of shit?" is the first thing Claire said. Vivian said no. "Then can you help me find my cat?" Claire burst into tears, but Vivian remained calm, and asked if she could take notes. That was how Claire knew that Vivian was a professional.

"Let me come over," Vivian said. "And look at some of

Rosemary's things. Then we can get started." They made an appointment.

The baby hadn't been sleeping well. Claire was sure he could sense that something was amiss. Could babies smell fear, or was that just dogs? Surely they had formed some kind of bond when Sebastian was in the womb, when Rosemary used to drape her thin black frame around Claire's rising middle. Before they moved to Cobble Hill, Claire and Matt talked about real estate as much as they talked about themselves. Who were they, they would ask: a one bedroom with an office? A half bath? Were they a decorative fireplace or a breakfast bar? When Claire got pregnant, things became clear. They were a two-bedroom, one-and-a-half bath co-op on the garden floor of a brownstone. Rosemary could lie in the sun, the bricks baking her black fur. They were a family of four. Everything was going to be perfect, just like in a magazine: glossy and impossible.

Vivian came over on a Thursday. They sat at the kitchen table and drank decaffeinated tea. Rosemary had been gone six days. Claire had Sebastian strapped to her chest, face-out. He was sixteen weeks.

"So how does this work," Claire said. She and Sebastian had the same green eyes, the same thin, dark hair. Claire was pleased that the baby looked more like her—was it fair the other way around? She couldn't imagine carrying a bowling ball for nine months just to have it come out looking like someone else. This was the point of having a baby: a tiny, growing mirror.

"Tea is good," Vivian said. She wrapped her hands around the mug and smiled. Vivian was small and had olive skin; she was from somewhere else, somewhere outside the five boroughs, even. Just moving to Brooklyn had been big for Claire. Her friends and whatnot. But Vivian was from even further afield. She had a scar on her arm from an old-fashioned inoculation. Claire had been careful about those with Sebastian, and now she wondered about everyone else's parents, how they could have been so negligent. She was sure that even then, there had been options.

Claire chose another tack. "Do you like the kitchen? We just had it redone. The travertine used to be marble. I think it looks more modern this way, don't you? It was so '80s. And the backsplash tiles were actually in a subway station. Somewhere in Brooklyn, I think. They were reclaimed." One of the few times that Claire's father came to the house, he promptly spilled a glass of Cabernet on the white slipcovers in the living room. Now she tried to keep people in the kitchen, where the surfaces were easier to clean. Vivian nodded patiently. "Let's talk about Rosemary," she said. Her eyes fixed on Claire's in a focused staring contest. She took a box of tissues out of her shoulder bag and put it between them, one fluffy Kleenex already poking through the top of the box.

"Okay," Claire said, "but before we start, I want you to know I still think this is all totally ridiculous."

"You called me," Vivian said. "Let's just see what I can do." She leaned back in her chair, patient. Sebastian kicked his feet with approval.

When Matt came home from work, Claire waited to see how long it would take him to remember that she'd had a date, that she'd done something with her day. It took almost an hour. He was practically asleep, and on his second glass of Sauvignon Blanc.

"Oh!" He said, instantly pleased with himself. "How was your yoga friend, whatshername?"

"Vivian." Claire crossed her arms. The baby was already asleep. She felt almost weightless without his solid body resting against her.

"Whaddid you girls do? Some chanting?" Matt made little peace signs with his fingers and closed his eyes. The TV barked something about the stock market and his eyes flipped back open. One thing Claire had actively wanted to avoid was The Dad Chair, which was inevitably at the head of the table, looking straight at the television. She hadn't noticed until Matt became a dad that this had, in fact, been waiting to happen for all five years of their relationship.

"No, no chanting."

"Huh, oh well. Have fun, though?" Matt didn't take his eyes off the screen. It was blue and pulsing, the visual equivalent of a shout.

"Yup. Sebastian likes her." Claire waited. Sure enough, as though she was watching her words flit through the air and slowly drift down into his ears, Matt turned her way.

"Sebastian?" he said, as though the name alone were a question.

Claire wanted to know how it all worked. She made Vivian

explain. Few of her clients worked regular hours, and so Vivian spent most of her days going from house to house. Not that she discriminated; she could just as easily go to their offices. There were often secretaries who would close the door. You'd be surprised who believed in what, given unforeseen circumstances. Guys in suits. The woman who cleaned the yoga studio. It took all kinds. Mostly though, Vivian admitted, it was women like Claire. Pretty and bored, with husbands who were usually somewhere else. Vivian didn't use the word 'bored,' but Claire heard it in her voice. It wasn't unlike therapy.

Everyone's first question was, Is he OK? Vivian looked at people's belongings, at their clothes, at the framed photographs on their desks and in their hallways. She'd pet the hairy, matted cushions, and the dented spots on the couch. She could always start there. Then the client would sit with their hands over their mouth, give the occasional nod, and try not to cry.

Sebastian's room was blue: cerulean, not navy. Nothing nautical. Nothing that would make him want to join the Army, or play with slingshots. The decorator had been very helpful in that regard, assisting Claire in the decoding of paint chips. People fought more in yellow rooms, everyone knew that. But there were other clues too. The color of the walls was as important as pre-natal classical music and talking through the belly-button. Sebastian was very lucky to have her. Claire was doing everything right.

Before the baby, Claire had held three jobs. The most recent job was as the deputy beauty editor at a women's magazine. Everyday she sorted through boxes of new products: lip glosses, skin creams, thickening sprays. Her office's windows faced Seventh Avenue. She'd had an assistant, a girl straight out of college who wore heels everyday just to answer the phone. Claire had loved her job. It had been up to her to identify the best; she was a tastemaker. There was a photo of Claire in every issue, and she'd demurred when the editor-in-chief asked to include a pregnant shot. In the magazine, Claire was forever thirty-three and a size four. No one wanted beauty advice from someone's mother. Sometimes Claire took out old issues of the magazine just to look at her photo, and do the wrong math: this baby couldn't be hers. Hers had been a phantom pregnancy, like a teenage girl in the 1950s, sent off to an undisclosed location while still small enough to fit into her normal clothes. This thought always made her smile.

Their second date at the kitchen table was more serious: Claire agreed to Vivian's terms. One hundred dollars per visit. Six visits minimum. No guarantees. Claire was sure they could negotiate that last part somewhere down the line, once Vivian understood what Rosemary meant to her, how much she really deserved her back. Claire was confident in her own abilities. She was very persuasive.

"How long had you been letting Rosemary outside?" Vivian's chair was angled towards the garden. Together, they watched a robin fly from branch to branch, its voice trilling upwards towards unseen friends.

"Since she was a kitten," Claire said. "She was always very independent."

Vivian nodded. "Mm hmm."

"Not in a stereotypical way, though," Claire said. "She was practically a dog. Always next to me. But when she wanted space, she took it." In the last week, Claire had often felt Rosemary's body brush against her bare calves, only to realize that it was a chair leg or Matt's socked foot, which she would immediately kick away.

"Of course not." Vivian held a stuffed cigar in both her hands, rolling it back and forth like a piece of Play-Doh. The cigar was Rosemary's favorite, Claire assured her. It had been an early present from Matt: the only one, in fact. Claire had kept that information to herself. If Vivian was good, she thought, she'd figure it out.

"And since the baby?" Vivian asked.

She was good.

The housekeeper was only there three days a week, and Claire didn't like to leave Sebastian with her for more than an hour or two at a time. Sometimes she went to the make-up counters at Barney's and Bloomingdale's just to see what was new. She'd review the products to herself and the salesgirls. "This one is a little sticky, don't you think?" she'd say, tapping a red stain across her lower lip. "This feels awfully thick. God, my pores are clogged already, can't you see that? Look, can't you see my pores getting totally clogged?!" The salesgirls would take turns responding, humoring her. Claire always cried in the taxi on the way home. New York was good for that, providing transportation and anonymity simultaneously. Some of Claire's friends from college had moved to Connecticut and New Jersey, and they were trapped. It was harder to drive and cry than to sit in the back behind a partition and just watch the streaky city go by.

According to Vivian, Rosemary was a people-cat who had been driven from her family by a mixture of anger and envy. Often, people didn't understand how to ensure their pets' happiness surrounding the arrival of a new addition. It was a common mistake. Just closing some doors in the middle of the night wasn't enough. Vivian said that she would meditate and get back to Claire when she had more information. Vivian was patient and explained the process. Clearly, she'd had to do it before. "I can tune things in and out. It's not like in the movies, where dead people talk and ghosts ride the subway. It's just another frequency, like on an old-fashioned radio, only all the knobs are in my head," she said. Claire got it. If Vivian sat still and kept her eyes closed, she might hear something new. She had to pay attention.

Black cats were bad luck; everyone knew that. Matt had been wary of Rosemary from the start. She was skinny and mean to everyone but Claire, and sulked loudly in the middle of the night when she felt that her needs were not being taken seriously. Matt said that they should get rid of her as soon as Claire got pregnant. If the cat woke *them* up at three in the morning, why wouldn't she wake the baby?

"What about when he starts to crawl," Matt said, "and starts getting kitty litter all over his hands and knees. Isn't that unsanitary?" He didn't seem to notice that they paid someone to clean the floors, cat or no. He floated the idea of a dog. Matt had always liked that idea: a boy and his dog. They could make it their Christmas card. Claire had been firm. They already had enough on their plates. It was a discussion for the future.

Claire stopped going to the post-natal yoga classes. It was too tempting, the thought of ninety minutes with nowhere she had to be. At first, she used the time to hang flyers with a black-and-white picture of Rosemary and her telephone number, along with the promise of a cash reward. Then she started to run.

There were paths through Prospect Park where she could have seen flowers and trees, but Claire preferred running straight down Court Street and over the Brooklyn Bridge. From her house, it was only three miles there and back. There were some women she passed who always ran with their strollers, the ones shaped like boomerangs, pushing their babies in front of them like so many carrots on so many sticks. Claire preferred to run alone. She liked it when her breathing evened out into a shallow pant, and her thigh bones felt hollow. Maybe that's where Rosemary had gone, inside. When she was pregnant with Sebastian, that internal connection had been her favorite part. She could feel him in ways that no one else could. His elbows, his feet. His hunger. It was better than having Matt around, or any of her girlfriends. Sebastian—they'd had the name from the very beginning—was closer. She imagined the cord between them as wide as the woven rope bracelets she'd worn as a teenager, inches thick, and heavy. When Sebastian actually arrived, they hung a sheet at her mid-section so that she couldn't watch them cut into her flesh and pull him out.

Matt, on the other side of the sheet, had been surprised by the amount of blood, the surgical nature of what followed. Claire was only surprised at how empty she felt with no one inside her, no one but herself.

When she first started to run, Claire would notice small aches, her shins, a hip. After a couple of miles, though, the aches would soften and vanish, leaving her body with a warm hum. It wasn't as if the pain had never been there at all, it was just as if the pain had changed shape, or gone slightly out of focus. Her sneakers would continue to hit the ground, one after the other, until the rest of her body seemed to float there, inches above the gray concrete. Some days, Claire would hit the Manhattan side of the bridge and just keep running. Once she made it all the way to Union Square before catching sight of the time outside a bank and turning around.

The doorbell rang and Claire was in the kitchen—too far to get there first. Matt beat her to it.

"Can I help you?" he asked, in the voice he used for homeless people and Jehovah's Witnesses. Matt had the square look of a hockey player, his jaw and shoulders both straight, thick lines. Next to him, Vivian herself looked like a skittish cat.

"I'm Vivian," she said, walking towards the doorframe. Behind Matt, in the dark of the house, Claire and Sebastian moved towards the door. Matt blinked; he clearly didn't recognize the name. "The psychic."

"The what?" Matt's voice was almost a laugh. He thought that she was joking. Claire's pace quickened; she barreled down the hall, Sebastian's legs bobbing up and down. She looked at Vivian and shook her head. *No.* Claire was now right behind Matt, peering over her shoulder. He turned to face her.

"Did you hire a psychic?" He was amused, not angry, but his voice was loud. Claire glanced up towards the street, clearly worried that passers-by would hear. "Is that what you do with your days? Ha!" Only parts of his face were smiling.

"She costs less than the reward, which you already agreed to, so I don't know what your problem is." Claire was hissing. She cupped a hand to her forehead and pushed her hair back. It was warmer with their three bodies so close together, Sebastian between them like a beach ball with arms and legs.

"What, Rosemary? Is that what this is all about? The fucking cat?" Matt's voice got even louder and roused Sebastian out of his half-sleep. His mouth widened, and at first nothing came out. The noise grew from nothing until it spilled out into the air: a siren. "Give me the baby," Matt said, and pulled Sebastian out of Claire's arms. He roared past her ear, and she winced, as if struck.

Empty-handed, the women walked back outside and sat on the front stoop. Half a block down, a single daffodil had raised its yellow head. Vivian pointed it out, and Claire nodded.

"I almost feel sorry for him," Claire said. She didn't have shoes on, and placed her palms over the tops of her feet, as though that would protect them from the ills of the outside world.

"I'm sure Sebastian will be fine." Vivian sat on the next step down and tucked her legs up against her chest. The sun warmed the parts of their hair.

"I meant my husband."

"Oh. Him, too." Vivian smiled. It was like being girlfriends, sitting this way. They could have braided each other's hair and sold lemonade, or smoked furtive cigarettes.

"It's just that, no matter how hard he tried, he's never going to love Sebastian enough. It's physical. I mean, I know that sounds bad, but how can he expect to feel what I feel?" Claire stared across the street at nothing in particular. Her jaw hung heavily, pulling her mouth slightly open.

"And how do you feel?" Vivian asked, following Claire's stare to the opposite sidewalk.

"I don't know," Claire said. She wasn't sure if this counted as one of their sessions, or if they were just having a conversation. "Like a rock. Or maybe like something at the bottom of the ocean." She stuck out her tongue and made a noise. "Maybe I should start going back to yoga." Claire picked up a twig and started poking her big toe.

"Do you want to know about Rosemary?" Vivian said, finally.

Claire inhaled. "Yes," she said, finally turning her face towards Vivian.

"Well," Vivian said, and started. She told Claire about how Rosemary had understood that it was her time, and that it would be easier on the family if she went away. Claire recognized the kind of story Vivian was telling her. It was the same kind of story she used to whisper towards her own belly-button, where Sebastian was still inside. It was a fairytale, full of hope. Vivian was telling her something she wanted to believe.

"So she's dead," Claire said, cutting Vivian off.

"Well, yes, I think so." Vivian looked startled. She wanted to keep talking.

Claire bent her knees and stood up, brushing off her jeans. "Okay," she said. "Okay." Then she turned around and went back inside. Vivian heard the locks click into place.

A MAP OF MODERN PALM SPRINGS

The Palm Springs airport was more outside than inside, all sun-soaked breezeways and squinting white people in golf shirts. I waited for my sister at the door to her gate, stretching my pasty calves into a patch of direct light, the first light of any kind my legs had seen all winter. It was February, and I'd only barely remembered to shave in preparation for the trip. Of course, Abigail would have noticed that first, my prickly legs. She wouldn't even have said anything—just given a long, slow look.

I rarely flew, but the trip from New York had been easy enough. I'd had a window seat, and the women sitting next to me had chatted amiably to each other the entire way about the fitness conference they were both attending that weekend. When she arrived, I'd tell Abigail all about it—the booths! The demonstrations! The great strides in moisture-wicking fabric! But no, Abigail wouldn't care about that. Abigail wouldn't even think it was funny. Once she'd started meditating, Abigail's sense of humor vanished. *Moisture-wicked right out of her body,* I thought, and started to laugh to myself, already goofy from the heat. I cupped my hands around my eyes and waggled my feet back and forth in my sneakers, making little semi-circles on the dusty concrete.

"What are you doing? You look like a crazy person, Dumbo." Abigail stood in front of me, blocking the sun. I looked up, my hand in salute position. My sister was coming from Los Angeles, a puddle jumper, if the desert was a puddle. She was already dressed for the weather, in loose, light layers that floated around her body like a hippie nimbus. Even her hair looked well-rested, her soft blondish curls bouncing up and down from her shoulders, sprung springs.

This was the first vacation of its kind: no parents (ours), no husband or kids (Abigail's). Just sisters. I couldn't remember whose idea it was, or how it came to pass that tickets were purchased and a hotel room booked, when clearly (it was already so clear) this should have been yet another generous, twinkling thought that floated away as soon as it was spoken aloud.

Abigail slung her bag off her shoulder and let it hit the ground with a gentle thud. She was six years older than me, and so many steps ahead that it hardly seemed we were on the same track. By the time Abigail was twenty-nine, my age, she was already married. Two years later, she had her first baby, and another two year later, her second. Abigail owned a house, a car, a swimming pool. She practiced yoga and made giant vats of her own juice and mayonnaise.

I stood up and let myself be folded into my sister's embrace. "Hi," I said, into Abigail's shoulder. "Welcome to California."

"I was already in California, Dumbo," Abigail said, pulling back. She held me at arm's length, gripping both shoulders for several seconds before letting go. My sister's face had all the elements of mine—blue eyes, long nose, pale skin—but arranged slightly differently, with a strong jawline that had come out of some deep corner of the gene pool. No one ever came out and said it, but it was the truth. I was forever a watery Abigail.

"Oh, right. Well, then welcome *me*," I said. I was sweating already. Was it always so warm here? Why hadn't we gone somewhere temperate, somewhere with things to do, and a thousand people to disappear into on every corner?

"It's so good to see you," Abigail said, scooping up her bag and pulling me back into her arms, shoving my face neatly into her armpit. "You're so skinny, I can hardly stand it." The damp cotton smelled like flowers that had started to decompose. It was probably Abigail's chemical-free deodorant, the kind that looked like a giant crystal, but I wasn't sure.

The rental car was small, so small they called it a compact, which sounded like a way to shame customers into spending more money, but Abigail didn't budge. It seemed pointless to offer to drive—I only barely had a license anyway, and driving Abigail would have been like driving our father, a perpetual Drivers' Ed class, with lots of fake brake pumping and wheel-grabbing. It was better just to let Abigail be in charge. Palm Springs was made up of golf courses, motels, and green-brown palm trees that stretched perilously into the bright blue sky. I'd forgotten my sunglasses and saw spots whenever I turned away from the window.

"So, how are Jack and Violet?" My niece and nephew both

had names for older children, for grown-ups. At two and four, it seemed like satire.

Abigail waved her hand in front of her face, moving it in a circle. "They're amazing! They're everywhere! You should see Jack, he's a little man. Running, talking, thinking all the time. He's on a soccer team. Which I wasn't sure about, you know, all the competition. But he really loves it, really loves it. And Vi! Oh, Vi." Abigail paused to look at me, the corners of her mouth pointing towards her chin. This was her Serious Face. Violet hardly spoke and liked staring at the ground. We all suspected there was something wrong, but didn't dare say so. "She reminds me of you. So quiet and careful. It takes her eons to do anything. Really such an artistic soul. You should come see them. It's been over a year, you know."

I unfolded the map from the car rental agency, which seemed to have only four streets on it, and realized I was holding it upside down. "Uh-huh," I said, and flipped it over before Abigail noticed. I was still lost. "Turn left on Alejo. I think." Single-level motor lodge motels lined every major street in town, and I couldn't remember which one was ours— Abigail had booked it, and I'd only had to say yes, to get on the plane, to show up. Even without the map, Abigail seemed to know where we were going, and made a few more turns, finally pulling into the parking lot at the hotel. The sign for the Orbit Inn was five feet high, orange, and shaped like a boomerang.

"Trippy," I said.

"Oh God," Abigail asked. "I haven't taken acid in so long. You don't trip, do you, Dumbo?" She gave me a look that was almost sympathetic, and heading towards conspiratory. She wanted me to say yes.

"No," I said. "I was just trying to be funny."

"Oh," Abigail said. "Right." She got out of the car and clicked the door shut. This was something I had chosen to do: try to be funny. It had been a year since I started improv classes, and six months since I started performing stand-up at a small but well-known theatre downtown. Inside our family, Abigail had always been the funny one, and she conveniently forgot that I was trying, that my failure was so guaranteed that it would be better if she ignored my efforts entirely.

My best bit was about Abigail. It was always changing, depending on the reaction from the audience, but I called it 'Older Sisters Are Pretty Much Nazis' and it always got a big laugh. It started with the way Abigail liked to lock me in her closet while she pretended we were playing hide and seek, but really she'd just leave me there all afternoon, until I was crying not only because I was afraid, but because my bladder was about to burst. From there I went to a bit about Abigail making me lick the bottom of her shoe in front of a large crowd on the school bus. But the biggest laugh of all was when I revealed that she was now a stay-at-home mother of two, responsible for the moral and ethical development of two human beings. It wasn't like Abigail had never done anything nice for me, though. At the very least, she'd made sure that I had the immune system of a New York City sewer rat, impervious to disease or poison.

The hotel room was big, with two queen sized beds along one wall, and a TV and dresser along the other. Abigail put her purse down on the bed closest to the bathroom.

"You don't mind, do you, Dumbo?" She was already unpacking, stacking up short piles of T-shirts and underwear.

"No, I don't mind," I said. I wasn't even sure what I was supposed to mind.

"It's just that I get up a lot, at night. I think it's from my maternal clock, you know, always thinking I'm hearing the kids. This way I won't wake you up." She dug both of her hands into her pulley-suitcase and pulled out four plastic baggies filled with travel-sized portions of all her various lotions and creams.

"They let you on the airplane with all of those?" I asked.

Abigail shrugged her left shoulder all the way up to her earlobe. "I told them they were breast milk."

I sat down on my bed and ran my hands over the quilted blanket. The room smelled like cleaning products and coconut. The air-conditioning was on, but I was still warm. Abigail hummed something to herself, and I started picking at my nails, pretending that I wasn't just watching her. I wanted to know what she had in her suitcase—not just how many pair of shoes but where she bought the shoes, if they were tight in the toe or the heel, what they were made out of.

When I looked up from the tip of my jagged nail, with its half-moon of black polish, Abigail was naked. I hadn't seen her without any clothes on since she was thirteen, or maybe even younger. She'd left for college when I was in the seventh grade, and it had been a long time since she'd let me in her room while she was changing, even on vacation. Her nipples were darker than mine, and pointed towards the ground. Her stomach was bigger, too, and protruded out from her body, almost like when she was pregnant, a full swooping belly that started at her pubic hair. There was a red, indented line going all the way around her waist from her underwear. She was putting on her bathing suit. Abigail looked up and saw me watching her, but didn't make any moves to cover her body more quickly, the way I most certainly would have done.

"Don't you want to go swimming?" She asked, wiggling from side to side to scooch her black one-piece over her hips.

"Sure," I said. "Yeah, let's go." I stood up and walked slowly to the foot of the bed, where I'd let my bag fall on its side. After righting it, and unzipping, I felt about for the slippery material and pulled out my suit. I hadn't worn it in nearly a year. The only place I ever went swimming was the YMCA, and I'd long since let my membership lapse. When I straightened up to step out of my shoes and socks, Abigail stared at me with her arms crossed over her chest.

"What?" I said.

"Nothing!" Abigail said. "Nothing!"

I slid my underwear down with my skirt still on, and replaced them with the bikini bottom. Then I turned around and faced the wall before pulling my shirt off over my head.

It was Saturday afternoon and the poolside recliners were almost all taken, with towels, tubes of sunscreen and paperback books left as placeholders while their owners took a dip. Abigail led us down a narrow shady alley between rows of recliners until she found two empty ones next to each other. She whipped off her gauzy cover-up and lay down on her stomach, her thighs rolling out to a resting position. I tucked myself into the seat next to her and put a towel over my face.

"I need sunglasses," I said. "It feels like my eyeballs are turning into hardboiled eggs."

"We'll get you a pair of sunglasses, Dummy," Abigail said through the plastic slats of the recliner, her face pointing straight down to the concrete. She moaned.

"Are you okay?"

"I'm amaaaazing," she said. "Look, I don't have any children! None! I'm hands-free!" She waved her hands on either side, and then lay them palm up beside her body.

The pool was split in half by a string of small white buoys, cordoning off the deep end from the shallow. On the shallow side, three sets of mothers and babies paddled around, the babies' chubby arms held aloft by inflated wings. The other end of the pool was full of young couples splashing each other while simultaneously trying to hold their drinks above their heads.

The heat was different than I expected. It wasn't like in Florida, where the minute I was outside the air-conditioning, my pores expanded like sponges. Here I didn't even notice I was hot until the sun was directly overhead, as though all the heat and warmth was transmitted directly from the rays themselves. Abigail's bathing suit had migrated into her butt crack, and I waited for her to tug it out. She didn't.

"Hey Lizzie," she said. Abigail only used my given name when she wanted something. "You think anyone around here would sell us some pot?"

I squinted at the people hovering around the edges of the pool. There were a couple of teenage boys at the towel stand.

One of them had a wispy goatee, the hairs making up in length what they lacked in quantity.

"Sure," I said. "I'll see what I can do."

When it was almost sunset, and she'd had enough of the plastic slats digging into her legs, Abigail decided it was time to go on a tour of Modern Palm Springs. She'd picked up a brochure at the desk. We put clothes on over our dry suits and hopped it the car.

The Visitor's Center lived in a building that had once been a gas station, with a swooping roof that came to a point way overhead, high enough for spaceships to dock underneath.

"We're at a gas station," I said. "This is part of the tour?"

Abigail slapped my wrist lightly, which stung nonetheless. "Don't be a pill." She paused, and looked through the window. A couple of white-haired ladies in crisply washed polo shirts came out, clutching unfolded maps. "You can wait in the car, if you want."

I rubbed my wrist. "Okay," I said, and did.

The tour consisted of a self-guided tour of about 75 modern houses and buildings, including the former gas station where Abigail bought the map. We started at the next nearest destination, a house with a name I didn't recognize. Abigail slowed down a few blocks away, and we pulled up in front of an address with a gated driveway and a ten-foot-high hedge all the way around it. On the other side of the gate, a gardener was using a leaf-blower. Abigail and her husband had a gardener, too. I wondered if she watched him work, or just left an envelope of money under the doormat. The only plants

I had were plastic.

"Wait, so this is the tour? Going around to look at houses you can't even see?" I said. Over the top of the hedge, a flat roof was visible. "It looks like everything else. You can't even see anything."

Abigail shook her head and rolled down her window, as if that was going to help. I stared at her while she stared at the invisible house. Tiny little lines formed a fan around the crease of her eye.

"I'm sure we'll be able to see the next one better. They can't all be like this. I'm not that crazy about Neutra, anyway," Abigail said, turning back from the house. She hit the button to roll up her window, stabbing it with her pointer finger until the window was all the way up. There were sweaty spots on her cheeks, and she whisked them away with her palm.

In fact, almost all of the houses on the map were similarly blocked from the street. The fold-out brochure, with its ten or fifteen color photographs of interior shots, held vastly more visual information. We drove by Frank Sinatra's house and a dozen others, seeing nothing more than gates and fences and hedges and maybe a slip of a house receding into the hillside.

"One more," Abigail said. "One more, and then I'm going back to the pool. This is absurd."

I nodded in agreement, though she would have called the tour off even if I'd protested. She had had enough. Despite the pumping air-conditioning, Abigail was flustered and sweating even more.

We picked the one called Elvis' Honeymoon Hideaway, though it had another name, too, and neither of us knew for sure that it was actually where Elvis and Priscilla had honeymooned. Everything in Palm Springs seemed to be surrounded by quotation marks, all the gas stations that had turned into tourist attractions and the Denny's that were now dining destinations for vacationing gay guys from San Francisco. Even Abigail and I were playing the part of happy sisters, when we were just two women captive in the desert.

The house was inside a small park—at least it seemed that way on the map, a green rectangle with fat white lines for streets. It took us a few wrong turns, but finally we were parked in front of the address, on a tiny cul de sac, with nothing blocking us but the owners' electric-blue Ford, which seemed far too modest for the house it stood before. The roof was peaked like the gas station, with two straight lines pointing high into the sky, only they were orange, and sat on top of a boxy teapot of a house. It was hideous.

"Elvis lived here?" I asked, checking the map for details I knew it didn't contain.

"No, just his honeymoon. At least that's what it's called. How am I supposed to know?" Abigail crossed her arms over the steering wheel and rested her chin on her wrists.

"It's really fucking ugly, huh," I said.

"So is Graceland," Abigail said, shifting the car into reverse.

The mustachioed kid at the towel stand not only had weed, he had mushrooms. I'd never taken them before, but it seemed like something Abigail would be impressed by, if I brought back something more serious. That night, we met in the parking lot of the motel next door while Abigail was talking to her children on the telephone. His name was Justin.

"You should go to Joshua Tree," Justin said. "Shrooms and Joshua Tree are like peanut butter and jelly."

"Or like peanut butter and bananas," I said. Justin passed me a joint, expertly rolled. He only looked like a slacker. "What do you do around here for fun? You know, when all the tourists go home?" I asked. The smoke hit the back of my throat like a brick wall, thick and heavy.

"Man, nothing. You're looking at it." We both looked around. The cleaning ladies carts weaved in and out of open doors, and all the cars in the lot were rentals. "Only the parking lot is empty."

"You know where I could get a pair of sunglasses?'"

Justin nodded and took two more hits in quick, sharp breaths. "Yeah, man. I can hook you up. One-stop shopping, you know? One-stop shopping."

The night was so dark it seemed imaginary—no lights, only stars. A cool breeze made its way through the palm fronds. Goosebumps appeared on my arms, and I rubbed them quickly. "My arms feel like alligator skin," I said, suddenly high.

"Oh yeah?" Justin said. He dropped the roach and crushed it under his flip-flop. Before I even knew what he was doing, his wispy goatee was tickling my chin, and his hands were cupping my boobs over my T-shirt. When he turned away, Justin stuck his hand out behind him, silently asking me to follow him. I took his hand and let him lead me back to an empty room in our hotel. There were no sheets on the bed, and I could hear a television blaring in the room next-door.

Before Justin peeled off my clothes, I said, "Who watches

TV on their vacation? Isn't that what you're supposed to do when you're bored at home?"

"You're funny," Justin said. And then I knew I'd let him do whatever he wanted.

The next morning, I went back to our room to take a shower and Abigail was already gone. I found her by the pool. She was lying on her back with a towel over her face and her straps hooked under her armpits.

"Hey," I said.

Abigail pulled down a corner of the towel, enough for one eye to peek out. "Bow chicka wow wow," she said, and covered her eye again. "I mean, good for you and all, but it wouldn't have killed you to let me know that you weren't, you know, dead." All of her blonde curls were piled on top of her head like an elaborate wedding cake.

"I had my cell phone on me. You could have called." I sat down next to her and looked at my arms. They had already passed through whatever tan zone they may have been in, and were now halfway to bubblegum pink. "I got us some mushrooms."

Abigail pulled the towel off her face completely, and struggled to sit up. There were fat red marks across the backs of her arms from the slats in the plastic chair. "Does that mean that you stayed out all night *with a drug dealer?*" She leaned forward, close enough that I could smell the lingering notes of her breakfast.

"I may have," I said, and turned towards the pool, waiting an extra beat for comic effect. Abigail gave a long, loud, hooting laugh, and then slapped my knee. Justin, with all of his twenty-two years and suntanned boredom, hardly seemed to qualify. Maybe I could work it into a joke—the only drug dealer I ever picked up sold drugs mostly at his former high school, and spent the rest of his time handing out chlorine-scented towels to pale tourists. A plane flew by overhead, and we both leaned back to watch the tiny object, no bigger than a bath toy.

Joshua Tree National Park was a forty-five-minute drive away, and the compact car got noisier and noisier the higher into the mountains we drove, as if in complaint. It was only ten in the morning—we figured we'd go, tool around, and be out of there before it was noon and so hot that we'd fry as soon as we got out of the car. Abigail had a water bottle, the stainless-steel kind sold at health-food stores, and I bought a big plastic one, which made her wince.

"I bet you don't even recycle," she said, shaking her head.

"They fine you if you don't," I said, which was true, but only if you put your trash out on the street on the days you were supposed to, and didn't just throw it away in the can on the corner like I did.

The park seemed, at first glance, to look like more of the same—knobby trees with prickly hands sticking out at odd angles, dry and dusty earth. Justin had told me what to expect. He'd said, "It's the desert. It's only exciting if you've never been there before." I tried to see everything out the window of the car through Justin's eyes: boring birds making noises at each other, boring lizards zipping across the cracked ground, boring boulders stacked on top of each other like an ogre's abandoned game of Jenga.

The map from the ranger station wasn't encouraging. *People have died here from preventable accidents*, it said. Abigail dug a dirty tissue out of her purse and blew her nose. "I think I need to go back to the allergist," she said. "Do you have allergies, Dumbo? It's all genetic, you know."

"Nope," I said, though I hadn't been to a doctor since I graduated from college, and had a runny nose every year from April through July. "All clear."

"Oh, that's lucky," she said, but I could tell she didn't mean it.

After a few miles, Abigail pulled into the first small parking area, which was empty. "Wait," she said, turning around in her seat to look behind her, and out the back window. "Let's take the mushrooms."

"Right now?" I wasn't sure if I'd been planning on taking them at all, and certainly not in the middle of the desert in the middle of the day, when one of us would have to drive the car back into Palm Springs while staying on the correct side of the highway. "Won't they make us hallucinate?"

"Oh, come on, Dumbo, it is *really* not that big of a deal. Just eat half if you're scared. John and I used to take mushrooms all the time. In a lot of cultures, it's really spiritual." Abigail held out her open palm.

It was hard for me to think of Abigail ever having been a child, despite the fact that there was massive photographic evidence to the contrary. There she was in overalls, smiling through her missing teeth! There she was in a two-piece swimsuit, careening down a slip-n-slide! There she was, arms raised over her head on a balance beam! To me, Abigail had always been an adult. She did everything I did so many years earlier—pre-school, summer camp, menstruating—that by the time I got around to it, it seemed like ancient, boring news, like something mimeographed and yellow at the bottom of a forgotten drawer. For my entire life, I had always deferred to Abigail's judgment, because it seemed impossible that a situation would exist where I would be right and she would be wrong, where she would come up short. And yet here she was, flapping her fingers back and forth, impatiently waiting.

"Okay," I said. "Fine." The little baggie with the mushrooms was somewhere at the bottom of my bag, and I leaned down and probed around blindly until I felt it. They were small, brown, shriveled-looking things, not at all like the mushrooms you would see on a pizza, which were the only mushrooms I ever ate. I pulled out two, and placed one in Abigail's twitchy fingers. She popped it in her mouth immediately, rolling her head back to wash it down with a gulp of water. I held mine up to my nose and sniffed. It smelled like something rotten and poisonous. Abigail opened her eyes and looked back at me.

"You take it?" she asked. She hadn't seen me tuck it back into my palm.

"Yup," I said. "Gross." I scrunched up my face in imagined disgust.

"Ha!" I'd never made Abigail laugh so much, and wondered if the drug's effects were instantaneous. "Okay," she said, opening the driver's side door. "Let's go interact with some nature."

Neither of us had hiking boots of any kind, but I was wearing sneakers, which at least had rubber bottoms. Abigail had on a pair of strappy leather sandals that wound around her ankles and tied in a bow at her calves. When I'd asked, she said she could always tell which trails were difficult, and which one old ladies could do in their wheelchairs. We would do the latter.

The loop was two miles, and took us immediately up a flight of stairs made of rocks and boulders. Was there a difference? It seemed easy enough, and I kept up with Abigail easily. In the places that were wide enough to walk two people across, we walked next to each other, and when the path narrowed, I fell back and followed her through. That was the way it worked.

"Dumbo, come look!" Abigail pointed at a gecko zipping across the ground, its body twitching quickly back and forth as it scurried to safety. I watched the lizard vanish into a crack between two rocks, jealous that it had found shade. There were voices above us, and we both turned to look. Three men were dangling by thick ropes, climbing up or down, I wasn't sure. They had helmets and caribeeners and would have loved to have a long conversation with Abigail about the master cleanse, I just knew it. "Meow," she said, as if she'd heard me.

I wanted to wait and see how long it would take, how much silence we would need, before Abigail asked me a question. Not if I was hungry, or if I was as sweaty as she was, but an honest-to-God question about my life. That she hadn't even followed up about Justin-the-drug-dealer seemed like a sorry indicator. We were somewhere about halfway through the two-mile loop when I realized what I wanted to do. I wanted to leave Abigail in the desert. It wasn't like she would have to sleep there—we encountered small groups of people every few minutes, and there were the hunky rock-climbers. If I left her, she would still be able to find someone, to get a ride back into town, get to the airport. I wondered what the desert would look like on drugs, if the bright blue sky overhead would start to darken and change, if clouds would appear and speak to her in languages she didn't understand. I wondered if all the creatures in the park would hear her cry out for me, and whether they would come running to her rescue. Maybe they would stay put, hearing it all in her voice, every mean thing she'd ever done in her entire life. There were foxes and rattlesnakes, animals that could hurt her if they wanted to. Maybe I would just let her get a few steps ahead at a time, until those few steps became a few more, and a few more. I might just go and sit in the car. Or I might drive away, find a gas station that actually sold gas, and keep going until I was home.

PEARLS

Jackie was from Newport, Rhode Island, which as far as Franny knew was Nowhere, Rhode Island. Even though Franny was from Brooklyn, they both felt like total rubes at Barnard, where all the city girls wore going-out clothes to English class just because they felt like it. Their dormitory room was exactly the same as all the others on the hall, narrow and spartan, perfect for two eighteen-year-old nuns. Jackie tried to spruce it up with some pictures she'd cut out of magazines, mostly models dressed up to look like Ali MacGraw. The two girls tried to do the same—sweeping bell-bottoms and collegiate sweaters. The effect was not great on Jackie, with shoulders as wide as an Iowan football player, or on Fran, who stood just over five feet and had to hem every pair of pants by several inches, sometimes cutting off the bells entirely.

Jackie's family spent most of the winter in Florida, and sometimes she was permitted to bring a friend. When she asked Franny to go to Palm Beach with them during the Christmas break, Franny was so excited that she punched Jackie in the arm. It took Mrs. Johnson three phone calls to convince Mrs. Gold that airplanes were safe, and then the tickets were booked, and Jackie packed all three of her swimsuits, knowing full well that Franny would want to borrow them.

There was the Breakers in Newport and the Breakers in Palm Beach. Franny didn't know the difference. They pulled up in the rented car and Jackie's father handed the keys to a kid their age wearing a jacket like Sgt. Pepper. The boy was tan and blond and Franny looked at him like he was made of ice cream. Jackie thumped her in the arm.

"Hey," she said. "You coming?"

Franny grinned. That's what Jackie liked about her: Fran wanted to be from Newport as much as Jackie wanted to be from Brooklyn. If Franny could have pushed a button and swapped lives with her, like in *The Parent Trap*, she would have done it in a heartbeat. They both scrambled out of the backseat and picked up their purses, letting the bellboys take the rest of the luggage on a golden cart the size of their dorm room.

The hotel room had two full-sized beds but the girls swiftly decided that it would be better to sleep in one and use the other as the depository for all of their belongings. Franny forced Jackie to hang up her fancy clothes and then complained that she didn't have anything that would suffer from staying folded. They lay on their stomachs and waggled their bent legs back and forth. The Atlantic Ocean lapped and crashed outside the window, which was open.

"I can't believe how warm it is here," Franny said. They'd stripped off their airplane clothes and were wearing only their underwear. Jackie wore white briefs she'd stolen from her father and a flimsy camisole. Franny wore a bra the size of

Cleveland, with latches and hitches that would have held up a lesser mountain range. Jackie was impressed. A breeze snaked in and slipped around their waving calves.

"Want to go to the beach?" Jackie was a great swimmer, and had been the captain of her high school team. Franny shook her head. "Or Worth Avenue? Or get some lunch?" It was only noon, and Jackie'd only eaten a banana for breakfast. Franny met the Johnsons at the airport with both of her parents, and the look on her face told Jackie that she would have rather committed ritual suicide. Jackie couldn't imagine she'd eaten much, either.

"Lunch," Franny said. "Immediately."

There was a good place nearby. It had the best shrimp cocktails, and was close enough to walk. Franny changed into one dress after another—she needed something that said *Florida*, she said. Jackie sat on the edge of the bed and sang songs to try to hurry her along, but could only remember the chorus to "Both Sides Now," and so was singing it in an endless loop, her deep voice occasionally muffled by a pillow. "I'm going to eat this," she said. But then Franny trotted out of the bathroom in a pink dress and bright, shiny lipstick and Jackie was happy enough to let it go.

Every street we passed started with *Sea*. Seabreeze, Seaspray, Seaview. "God," Franny said. "They really got creative."

Jackie held her hands up to shield the sun from her eyes. "Tell me about it." After every block, the ocean appeared, a little window of blue. She could tell that Franny wanted to look, and walked slower. In her hand-me-down madras shorts and plain white T-shirt, Jackie felt like Franny's older brother.

She still had a swimmer's body; her shoulders were as wide as a man's, if not wider, and stretched and moved as she walked, like giant wings. Jackie's whole body was taut and boring, a straight line, and Franny's was wiggly. Everyone they passed on the street turned to look at her, and Jackie couldn't blame them. Franny moved her bottom from side to side with every step, like she was Fred Astaire dancing with an invisible Ginger Rogers, always pushing her backwards in those heels.

"You will come in the ocean, won't you?" Jackie asked.

"Will you save me if I drown?" Franny replied.

Jackie nodded. "Sure," she said. "Why not?"

The restaurant had white tablecloths and painted murals and a long bar filled with girls their age and their fathers or husbands. Jackie looked at Franny, ready to bolt, but she just sailed through the crowd, as if she were walking into their bathroom at school with her towel slung over her back. The maitre'd seated them at a table overlooking Worth Avenue, where they could watch women window-shopping while their patient chauffeurs trailed them like the world's worst secret service.

Jackie didn't even need to look at the menu. "Two cokes, one shrimp cocktail, two BLTs, please," she said, then looked up at Franny. "Is that okay?" Franny thought it was hysterical that she was Jackie's first Jewish friend, and Jackie still had tiny panic attacks when she was confronted by something that struck her as a Jewish Issue. Bacon was one of them. She didn't know enough to worry about the shrimp.

"It's fine," Franny said.

The waiter came back with two tall, slim glasses of fizzy

Coke, straws bobbing happily. They both lunged forward and sucked, the sugar gliding across the roofs of their mouths and then all the way through their veins.

"I love Florida," Franny said, and right then, Jackie did, too.

The reason Jackie's family stayed at the Breakers every year was for the Preservation of Newport Society's Pearl of the Sea Ball. Jackie hated wearing skirts and shoes with heels and so she started planning their exit strategy as soon as they were in the hotel room, Jackie pretending to be totally unconscious of Franny's excitement. She tried to tell her everything she hated about the ball: there was an orchestra. There was a seated dinner. There were boys from all over the country, slick with money. Rockefellers. Kennedys. There would be photographers from the Shiny Sheet, the same photographers who took pictures of Teddy when he was too drunk and had his arms around every woman at once. Franny's eyes got wider and wider and Jackie knew she'd said the wrong thing. There was no way they were going to miss a minute of it.

The Johnsons, Jackie's parents, had real first names, but almost nobody used them. Her father's name was Edward, and her mother's was Elizabeth, though other women tended to call her other things: Bitsy, Betsy, Betty. This had long since seemed strange to Jackie, but Franny raised an eyebrow every time somebody called her something new. Jackie's mother would kiss them on both cheeks, no matter what they'd called her. She went with the girls to the pool, claiming she just wanted some sun, but Jackie knew she wanted to keep an eye on them. Jackie spent most of her time diving off the highest board and ignoring her mother's requests to talk to other children. She told Franny they'd been kidnapped. They were hostages.

The shallow end was long enough to sit in, and Franny stretched her legs out. That way, she said, the sun could continue to have direct access to the largest number of pores. Every few minutes, Jackie would swim past, her goggled eyes open and unblinking, leap out of the pool, and run back around to the diving board. This was something Jackie knew Franny liked about her: dogged enthusiasm.

"Hey!" she said as she jogged around the bottom lobe of the pool. It was shaped like an eggplant, they'd decided. A gigantic eggplant filled with chlorine. "Jackknife!" Since Franny didn't know the name of any dives, Jackie had to make her own requests. Behind her, Jackie could hear her mother made a small groan at the noise they were making.

"Jackie the Jackknife," Franny said, seconding the motion with as much decorum as possible. She wanted Jackie's mother to like her. There were countless other girls the Johnsons could have brought in her place: Jackie'd shown her photo albums filled with pictures of friends from Portsmouth Abbey. She knew their names by heart: Susan and Laura and Barbara and Jane. Franny looked most like Jane, who also had dark hair and was small. Jackie's mother didn't like Jane, though, and so she'd invited Franny instead. When Franny asked why Jackie's mother didn't like her, Jackie told her it was because she was a "bad influence," which meant that Jane smoked and drank too much. Franny didn't ask more than that. Jackie turned around and waved at her mother and Franny, two sunny bodies. A waiter was bending down to set a drink on the small table next to her mother's lounge chair. She waved back, her pink nails little kisses in the air.

When Jackie'd made it back to the far end of the pool, the stem of the eggplant, she bounced up and down on the diving board. Her swimsuit was black and slick as a seal's pelt, and with the goggles, she felt like a Russian spy. Franny pushed herself off the wall and doggy-paddled out into the middle of the pool. She could see Jackie watching, or at least she thought she could. It was hard to tell with the goggles.

Before Franny could even yell up and alert Jackie to her newly water-bound presence, Jackie leapt up and did a forward flip. Her head was up, and then it was down. Her feet were down, and then they were up. She could feel her body fold in half, and then open up as straight as a pencil, into the water in one motion. Jackie loved to dive. If she could have stayed underwater forever, she would have. My water baby, that was what her mother used to say. My water baby.

Franny's legs looked like two white pillars. Her toes scraped against the bottom of the pool. Jackie swam as close as she could, and then grabbed Franny's left shin and gave it a tug. Jackie could hear Franny scream, even from under the surface. She popped up next to Franny, laughing, and then lifted the goggles off her eyes and moved them onto her forehead. There were deep indentations in her skin where the goggles had been.

"You look like you got into a fight with an octopus," Franny said.

Jackie spat out a mouthful of pool water. "What do you

think is down there?" she asked, gesturing with her right ear.

"Octopus!" Franny said, and before she'd finished saying it, Jackie was on top of her, underneath her, behind her, swimming like a fish, her hands two tentacles, just for Franny. She screeched, in spite of herself. Jackie hoped that her mother had gone to the ladies room.

The day of the Ball, they were booked. Mrs. Johnson made the three of them appointments to get their hair done. Jackie huffed and puffed through it all: the rollers were too hot, the hairspray stung her eyes. When they were back in the hotel room, her mother started to loom over Jackie's face with a mascara wand. She actually screamed.

"I can do it," Franny said. Jackie could tell that Fran was trying her hardest not to be ready too early. Her dress, on loan from Jackie's mother, lay flat on the bed, but her hair was done, her make-up, everything. Jackie'd loaned her a string of pearls, and she fingered them gingerly. They looked better on Franny.

"Yes," Jackie said. "Let Franny do it, Mother. We'll meet you in your room in half an hour, okay?" Mrs. Johnson already had her dress on and didn't look inclined to wait. "Or we'll meet you and Dad at the bar, how's that?"

"A gimlet doesn't sound like a *terrible* idea," her mother said. "Fine. You girls hurry up, though. I won't be late." Her skirt was the color of sea foam and pushed out from her body as though held up by tiny creatures. It was satin, the kind of thing you had to know you wanted, because they didn't sell it in every store. Not even at Bloomingdale's. She walked sideways so not to muss herself and closed the door behind her.

"Jesus," Jackie said. Another Jewish Issue word. She winced.

"Jesus," Franny said back. They smiled.

Franny guided Jackie backwards until she was sitting on the closed toilet seat. She sat next to her on the lip of the bathtub. They were wearing their slips, peach and white and slippery. She moved her make-up bag into her lap.

"Okay," Franny said. "Hold still."

Jackie closed my eyes.

"Your hair is so much poufier than normal," she said. It was true. The lady in the salon had somehow teased an extra four inches out of Jackie's hair. "You look pretty."

She kept her eyes closed. "Not as pretty as you are," Jackie said.

Franny laughed a little, even though she knew Jackie wasn't joking. She was prettier; everyone knew that. But there was something in Jackie's voice that was different. She'd told Fran before that she thought she was prettier, but always in a jokey, self-deprecating way. This time, Jackie said it like she wanted to kiss her. Which she did.

Here are all the boys Franny let kiss her before going to Barnard: Samuel Epstein, who was two years ahead of her at Midwood and immediately lied about her to all his friends; Josh Schwartz, who was almost as short as she was, and had a slippery tongue; Barry Weinstein, who was soft around the middle and touched her with the gentlest hands she'd ever felt, until now.

Here are all the boys Jackie ever let kiss her: zero.

She kept her eyes closed. Jackie didn't know if Franny found her mouth, or the other way around. One of them had moved closer to the other, or they both had, and Jackie could feel Franny's mouth in all different parts of her body: her ribcage, where it was vibrating against her chest, and in her underwear, twitching like someone had flipped a switch. Jackie slipped her tongue past Franny's lips and teeth, and there was a shudder somewhere inside her that she could feel. If Franny'd opened her eyes, she would have seen Jackie's eyes open, too. But Franny kept her eyes closed, as though that would ensure that they would laugh about this later, the way girls laugh when they're with their friends and they've just said something so deeply personal that they had to look at each other in a new way, to recalibrate what they'd previously taken for granted.

When they finally pulled apart, slow as taffy, their chins were red, as though they'd been mining their pores for blackheads. The bathroom mirror stared back at them, agape. Franny put her hand to her mouth, and Jackie did the same, Simon Says.

"Well, are you gonna put that mascara on me or what?" Jackie said, her face now pulling into a sideways grin. The small bathroom smelled like sweat and perfume and possibility. Franny plunged the mascara wand into the bottle a few times and then leaned forward, moving her hands back to Jackie's face. She shut her eyes slowly and evenly, as docile as if she'd been hypnotized. If Franny'd snapped her fingers, Jackie would have done anything she said. She could have whispered.

The ballroom made Rockefeller Center look like Times Square, seedy and filled with prostitutes. The walls were covered with red and gold silk, and above their heads, chandeliers twinkled like enormous diamond rings. There were round tables circling a dance floor, and the orchestra was already playing: Rodgers and Hammerstein. Jackie recognized the song. All around them, people were having the polite kind of talk that sounded like falling leaves, small crunches and murmurs. All the men wore tuxedos and bow-ties that matched their wives' dresses. The wait staff from the hotel restaurant was dolled up—young men Jackie recognized from the pool walked by carrying platters of champagne glasses. Inside, in the relative dark, their tans made them look like silent film stars, with features so easily translated into black and white.

"Why didn't I bring a camera?" Franny said into Jackie's ear. But of course, there were photographers, and flashbulbs, and for the first time, Jackie hoped that one of them would catch her, that maybe one of the photographers would take a picture of their arms around each other's waists and only they would know why they were smiling.

Franny couldn't stop looking at Jackie, which she knew from her peripheral vision. Whenever Jackie actually turned to look back, Franny would turn away, cheeks brighter than any man-made blush. Mrs. Johnson cupped her hand around Mr. Johnson's bicep as they entered the room. As far as Jackie could tell, time had stopped and there was no other party on earth, no other dinner, nothing that she cared about outside this room. She wanted to sit at the table and fill out her dance card with just one name over and over again, *Franny Gold, Franny Gold, Franny Gold.*

The table was close to the band, good seats. Mrs. Johnson

had pearls in her ears and a pearl on her finger. Jackie's own set was still strung around Franny's neck, flat against her collarbones. All around the room, women were just as decked out. Jackie wondered how many pearls were in the ballroom, if there were more pearls than in a hundred miles of the Atlantic Ocean. The three women sat down simultaneously, like a ballet corps, moving individually but with the sense to do it in unison.

"So, Franny, sweetie," Mrs. Johnson said. A waiter appeared behind her and put champagne glasses in front of them all, in between the gold chargers and the floral centerpieces with their dramatic spikes of red and white. Everything seemed native and wild. "Are there any boys up there at Barnard? Jackie never told us if you had a boyfriend."

She could see Jackie's neck, her cheeks, her chin. She could smell the kisses from two seats over. She wasn't a mother, she was a bloodhound.

"Franny goes out with tons of boys, Mother," Jackie said. "Tons. The Columbia Lions? All of them. The whole team." She shook her head in mock-disapproval. Franny's dress had cap-sleeves; Jackie wondered if they were both sweating so much, or if it was just her.

"No," Franny said, turning to face Mrs. Johnson. "No boys. At least not right now."

There were boys at Columbia, boys who would call and call and call, but Jackie couldn't picture any of their faces. She picked up her glass and held it high, her arm straight out and triumphant. "To Franny," Jackie said, "the pearl of the sea!"

Jackie's parents, Mr. and Mrs. Johnson, Edward and

Elizabeth, Ed and Bitsy, Bitsy and Bootsy, Bippity Bobbity Boo, everyone in the room seemed to raise their glass, and there was a booming inside Jackie's chest that would have made the ocean turn green with envy. She and Franny danced with each other and with her parents and with people who looked like they were bored out of their minds. Franny talked about Newport as though she'd been there a hundred times, and really, it was just a matter of changing her address with the post office. Jackie talked to old men about their sailboats and old women about their daschunds. When the party was winding down, Jackie's parents toddled off to their room and she and Franny ran for the beach with their shoes in their hands.

The hard, wet sand looked dark against their bare feet, like city concrete. Jackie ran fifty yards in her dress, the hem hiked up around her waist with her white slip taut against her thighs. She pictured Franny on Broadway, all those boys fading into the background. When Jackie stopped running, the girls stood there for a moment and stared at each other in the dark. Jackie could make out Franny's hair, which was starting to frizz in the humidity, and her dress, puffy under her arms like a barrel. Her feet were still mostly clean; Jackie's were speckled with sand and dirt. Above them, the Breakers looked like it had been carved out of a cloud, all smooth, all white. The ballroom was still lit up; the orchestra continued to play. Tired dancers could have walked to the window and seen them there, two ghost-girls. Jackie let go of her dress with one hand and waved, inviting Franny further away from the line of vision.

But Franny didn't move. What was down the beach? What would she do once she made it there? Jackie thought of the faceless boys on Broadway, and the way that Franny would have run to them, without even giving it a second thought, just because they were handsome and tall and exactly what she'd always imagined she would have. Jackie hadn't imagined that, not ever. She'd only imagined a girl like Franny kissing her back and meaning it. The longer they stood there, the more Jackie knew that Fran understood what she had never told her. That it wasn't a game. Now she could guess why Jane hadn't been invited along, why she had been chosen in her place. The kiss in the bathroom had not been Jackie's first, of course not. There were so many things Jackie wanted Franny to do, and one of them was fly across the sand, into the legion of girls like Jackie and Jane, not caring if her borrowed dress was torn to pieces in the surf. Jackie could have made a flying leap, an Olympic leap, right from where she stood into Franny's arms. She could have spun her out and in, out and in, until their arms were tired and so they'd use their mouths instead. But that was not what she wanted; even in the dark, that much was clear. Franny's face was blank and white. She was shivering. By the time Jackie started walking back towards her, her shoulders had collapsed for a few steps, and Jackie turned towards the ocean, offering Franny her profile so that she couldn't see her face. Jackie didn't stop when she reached her. Instead, Jackie pointed her body back to the hotel and said, "Well, you coming?" They flew back a few days later and never talked about the trip again.

ABRAHAM'S ENCHANTED FOREST

Old rides were easy to come by if you knew where to look. Places went out of business all the time. Abraham drove to Pennsylvania and Ohio to check out people's old Scramblers and Whack-a-Moles and Zip-Dee-Doos. If Greta was out of school, she went with him and gave her opinion on the rusting metal giants. She was sixteen now and could be trusted with important decisions. He rarely bought anything, though. Most of the time he'd come home and say, You know what? I've got an idea! Then he'd vanish into his shop for a few hours or a few days and come out with something strung together with pieces of old tires. All of the attractions at the Forest were homemade except for the lonely Ferris wheel, which poked dramatically over the tree line. There was a guy in Big Sur who carved things with a chainsaw, and he and Abraham had some kind of deal going. It had something to do with weed. Every now and then a truck would pull up and deposit a burl dwarf or wizard or unicorn, and there'd be something else inside, too. Abraham liked it when things looked like they could have occurred organically, like when a tree stump looked enough like a miniature castle to label it as such, but you'd still have to squint and maybe put in some windows and turrets in your head.

Greta knew that things were confusing on purpose.

The Enchanted Forest was an actual place, that's why lots of people stopped. On the map, there was a small triangle of green, labeled *Enchanted National Forest and State Park*, and Abraham's Enchanted Forest roadside attraction was on the highway headed in that direction. Before Greta was born, her parents Abraham and Judy had made enough signs to divert even the most dedicated of road warriors. *Look out, goblins ahead! Magical pony crossing! Entering Fairy Dust Area! Food! Rides! Unexplainable phenomena! Visit the Enchanted Forest, Five Miles!* His goal was to be the Northeast's answer to Wall Drug and South of the Border, but to actually give people a good reason to stop. Sure, he wanted them to pay admission, but more than that, he wanted to give them a worthwhile experience. He wanted to give them poetry and apple pie, the good kind of Americana. He and Judy had bought the land for nothing and then built the whole Forest from scratch, except for the trees. Greta knew that tourists considered the Forest a rip-off; after all, it was mainly a path through big old trees with some plaques telling you to look out for some imaginary thing, a Ferris wheel, and a place to eat lunch. But she also knew the truth: most people didn't look hard enough.

Apparently, you could see the upper rim of the Enchanted Forest's Ferris wheel all the way from New York City, which was thirty miles south. At least that's what Abraham liked to say. He was big-bellied and big-voiced and liked to say a lot of things. Sometimes Greta made lists in her spiral notebook. *Today, Abraham made a speech about different ways to reuse plastic water-bottles and it lasted for twenty-six minutes. Almost all of the ideas involved using way more plastic. What if no one wants to go inside a Trojan horse made of garbage?* In her sixteen years, she couldn't remember ever calling her father by anything but his first name. Abraham's enormous gray-and-white speckled beard was reason enough.

Greta's parents met in 1975, back when things were cheap. Her mother, Judy, was driving across the country in an old school bus with her then-boyfriend, who was a candle maker. The boyfriend—Greta could never remember his name, no matter how hard she tried—would set up camp somewhere and make candles to sell them at craft fairs and farmer's markets, and then, when he'd made enough money to last a few hundred miles, off they'd go. The problem was, one day the bus wouldn't start, and he decided he'd rather keep moving than stick around and make more candles. He gave Judy the bus and the buckets of wax and all the spools of heavy string for the wicks, and he was gone. For the next month, Judy and the bus sat in the parking lot and made candles on the asphalt. That was until she met Abraham. The way he liked to tell it, Abraham fell in love with the bus first, then Judy. It was a win-win situation.

The old, yellow bus now sat on the edge of the Enchanted Forest parking lot, as though a crowd of fifth-graders was on an endless field trip. They'd had it towed. You couldn't see much of the Forest from the parking lot; that was the point. You had to pay your money before you saw exactly what you were paying for. It was always fun when the lot was full—when she was little, Greta would wander in between the parked cars, weaving in and out, trying to count all the states from the license plates. Every now and then there was something exciting, like California or Colorado or Alaska, but mostly it was New York, New Jersey, Connecticut. All the ones she could spell without writing them in the air with her finger.

Of course, these days if the lot was full enough to have cars from Alaska, it meant that Greta was supposed to be inside, taking tickets or bussing tables or walking around smiling at people. She was supposed to be a fairy. Judy'd sewn her some wings. The costume really wasn't so bad. Greta could wear whatever she wanted as long as she had on the glittery wings, which she could put on and take off like a gossamer backpack. Most of the time, Greta put them on over her T-shirt or sweatshirt, depending on the weather. They were adjustable. Here's what Greta liked to wear: normal clothes. Not the kind that the popular girls wore, the ones whose parents had moved from the city, with brand names glistening off their breast pockets and waistbands, but the kind of clothes you wouldn't think twice about. That was her goal: to blend. The wings made it more difficult, but when she was at home, what was the point? There was no one to convince.

During the off-season, the long months between September and May, Abraham made money by going into local public schools and libraries and doing readings as Walt Whitman. He wore his cleanest clothes and a hat, though the beard and the voice were the real selling points. People would stand up and applaud, except for the small children, who would cower behind their parents' legs and occasionally burst into tears.

The tenth grade had read *Leaves of Grass* in English class that spring. Greta knew what was coming. The school wasn't big; everyone else knew, too. The teacher probably assigned the book because she'd seen Abraham do his shtick at the Enchanted Forest Public Library. High schools were always a joke in May, no matter where you were. The seniors were already into their colleges or technical schools or had jobs at the mall, and the juniors could see the light at the end of the tunnel. For everyone else, it was just the looming summer, and the sunlight, and the tanning lotion. During the year, it was easy to pretend that she had dreamed up the Forest and her parents and that, really, she had a normal house and a sister or two and a neutered dog, but once the summer was underway, it wasn't so bad. Abraham was funny when she had no one to compare him to.

Lincoln High School sat in the middle of the town proper, which was a fifteen-minute bus ride down Route 17 from the Enchanted Forest. People had started getting their learner's permits, and riders were dropping like flies, but Greta didn't mind. She couldn't imagine what kind of car Abraham would help her buy. The school bus, at least, was neutral.

He'd beat her to school somehow, despite the bus' head start. When Greta pulled open the heavy door to the main corridor, people were already giggling in a way that was impossible to misunderstand.

"Ahoy, matey," a boy from her geometry class called out. There was a portrait of Herman Melville in the mall's Barnes and Noble, and the beard was similar. She nodded and kept walking, holding her book bag tight against her chest.

Abraham's voice reached her first. It was "O Captain, My Captain," and it was coming from the direction of the cafeteria. Greta knew most of the big hits by heart, not on purpose, just because the house wasn't that big and Abraham liked to practice. Greta took a minute to picture Abraham in his Walt Whitman outfit, standing in front of the hot food trays. There were three bays for food—gross, grosser, and grossest. She usually ate from the first one, the salad bar. Greta imagined Abraham sticking his chubby finger into the plastic bucket of Italian dressing, and picking up a handful of cherry tomatoes without using the tongs. He loved cafeteria food. She knew that Abraham would stick around to eat, either before or after he spoke to her class, still wearing the Whitman outfit, and undoubtedly still in character. Greta could picture all the nerdy, bookish kids loving him, and crowding around his table. They would all look make-believe and pale next to him. They would slop up their applesauce and macaroni and cheese and not believe their luck. Abraham could do that to people, make them feel important, like they had something interesting to say. She took a breath and rounded the corner, her sneakers squeaking on the glossy red tiles. She looked through the glass-paned door at her father.

Abraham, or rather Walt, wasn't just standing in front of the lunch trays. One of his hands held aloft a slotted metal spoon, and the other was clamped over his heart. His eyes were closed. It was only the middle stanza. Greta closed her eyes, too, and waited for it to be over. The room was quiet aside from her father's voice and the clinking of cheap, school-issue flatware. There was going to be applause, and laughter. The ratio seemed unimportant.

Judy was in charge of the restaurant, which had a lunch counter and five tables, too small for the busloads of Japanese tourists.

In season, there was always a line out the door. Everyone paid cash and bussed their own tables—it was part of the appeal. Greta's favorite part of the entire Forest was her mother's apple pie. Some writer had mentioned it in a guidebook once— *You've Got to Eat This!*—and now people drove out of their way just to order a piece. In July and August, Judy baked fifteen pies a day. She'd been almost forty when Greta was born; Abraham was a decade older. It was some kind of miracle, Judy liked to say. "My tubes were all going the wrong way," she told Greta. "You were the only one who knew where to go."

The restaurant was painted green both inside and out, with fake vines winding their way up the walls in between the tables. Judy had drawn each of the leaves individually, so they were all slightly different, like snowflakes or the wooden creatures lining the path to the door.

"What do you think about a strawberry pie today, honey? Or maybe something with only red ingredients? So you were never sure what you were eating?" Judy set a fork and a knife at each place setting. It was still early enough in the season to experiment. Later in the summer, people would complain. Greta watched her mother bend over the tables, stretching her small back. She didn't wear any theme clothing, only stuff you could order from the L.L.Bean catalog. When her hair was loose, it hung down to the middle of her spine, but it was never loose during the daytime. Everyday, Judy twisted her hair into two long braids and fastened them to the top of her head with bobby-pins. Her hair was beginning to be more gray than brown. The effect was something like an aging Swedish milkmaid. It was her only concession to the fairytales happening around her, in her pies, on the walls.

"Sure, Mom." Greta had Abraham's body and Judy's face. She was taller than her mother by eight inches, and sometimes Judy still seemed surprised to have given birth to something so big and patted her daughter on the shoulder, shaking her head. Their faces were the same, though. Small ovals with tight brown eyes, and plump, pale lips. Greta liked that they looked similar—it was proof that there were some things in the world more powerful than Abraham. "Red pie sounds good."

"It could be 'Rose Red Rumble'!" Judy said, excited. It was good to give things theme names; that made people feel like it was worth three dollars a slice. The apple pie was called 'Sleeping Beauty's Revenge.' Judy and Greta wrote most of the fables that appeared on plaques around the property. They retold fairytales, sometimes with two different versions, Disney or Grimm. Greta had always preferred the Disney versions, which appalled her parents. Abraham would rail for hours against the dumbing-down of Cinderella. It was nothing without the bloody toestubs, he said, nothing at all. When Greta was little, she'd let her father dip her feet in red paint and then run, screaming, through the crowd.

In June, when people started to pile into their cars and RVs and station wagons, Greta came up with an attraction of her own: Who Wants to Kiss a Fairy? It was located behind the dining room or a little ways into the woods or wherever else no one usually went. She didn't charge; that would be gross. Instead, she kept an eye out for interested parties, and gave them The Look when it was time. There weren't very many boys who came to the Enchanted Forest and looked like they deserved a vacation fairy: the blond from Massachusetts with all those sisters; the tall, tan one from Florida who was alone with his mother; the funny one with the red hair who was soft all over. Most of the boys who came to the Forest just glanced at her boobs in the fairy costume and didn't even say hello.

It was only kissing, nothing gross. The blond one was the first. He was reading about Jack and the Beanstalk underneath Beanstalk's Ladder, the tallest tree in the Forest. Greta sidled up next to him and plucked at her wings, which she put on backwards, so that they were growing out of her chest, a concession to the boredom of the endless summer days. The blond blushed and didn't say hello, but she could tell that he was interested. It was a silent flirtation. They both looked around the corner, where his mother and three sisters had already scurried. A blond head soared above on the Ferris wheel. They had at least five minutes.

If the Enchanted Forest were in a movie, they'd always be playing Bob Dylan or Van Morrison or maybe even Leonard Cohen in the background. Greta thought about that a lot. Sometimes when she was taking a shower or helping her mom in the restaurant, she'd imagine what kind of scene it would be, and what would be playing to set the mood. Most of the day would end up in a montage; very rarely were things important enough for a whole scene. Her favorite movies were the ones where people just did normal stuff: go to school dances, eat dinner with their parents, take walks and talk to each other about their problems. The point was, no one in the movies ever seemed to realize how good they had it. No one ever lived on the side of the highway with Walt Whitman and a bunch of wooden dwarves.

Abraham was trying to fix the Hall of Mirrors. It was the gardening shed until he took it over. It was too close to everything else not to be a part of the tour, he said. Then you tell me where I'm going to put my shovels, Judy said back. The shed was too small to fit more than five or six people at once, four if one of them was Abraham.

"Don't you think you should come up with something different to call it? Like, if you're calling it a hall, don't you think it should have a hall?" Greta sat on the ground next to her father's toolbox, which wasn't a box at all, but a stained canvas bag.

"People come for the attractions, babygirl. It's all how you present your case." Abraham had briefly considered going to law school, several times. His voice boomed from inside the shed. It was missing a roof, so it wasn't even a shed anymore, it was just a bunch of walls.

"I see," she said, lying down in the grass. The cool, flat flagstone path crossed under the backs of her knees. Greta looked straight up at the sun and imagined that she was tied to railroad tracks. If she stayed put long enough, someone was sure to come along to rescue her.

"Hand me the hammer, will you?" Abraham stuck his hand out of the hole where the ceiling should have been.

Greta rolled onto her side and blinked enough times to have the world make sense again. The clouds were solid masses of marshmallow Fluff, the kind that Judy would never let her eat. If she lived inside a television commercial, she would be able to reach up and take a pinch. Greta extended two fingers and tried, squeezing nothing but dumb, blue air. "I'll be right on it, Chief," she said.

Every year, during the high season, Abraham hired Joe from the library circulation desk to come and work the Ferris wheel. Joe was seventy and had fought in a war—Greta wasn't sure which one. He wore an Army-green cap with a short bill to keep the sun out of his eyes, although his freckled and sagging skin suggested decades of reckless summers and melanoma.

Joe stood by the gate to the Ferris wheel. He took his job very, very seriously. There were safety issues, he knew, and he was in charge. Abraham liked him because he never smiled, which Abraham thought was hilarious.

"Afternoon, Joe," Greta said. She plucked at her left wing. It was sticky outside, and the straps adhered to her bare skin.

"Greta." Joe nodded, and continued to stare straight ahead.

People were milling around the Forest, as much as one could mill around. There was a single path, and arrows pointed you in the right direction. Unless you hopped a fence or consciously disobeyed Abraham's 'Trespassing is for trolls' signs, there was only one way to go. But people seemed to like it anyway, at least most of the time. Women usually took pictures of their children standing next to the wooden dwarves outside the Snow White cottage. Sometimes they even climbed onto the tiny wooden beds, even though they weren't supposed to. Greta never stopped them. Teenaged siblings shoved one another. Nothing out of the ordinary.

Greta's room was in the back of the house, and looked out into the trees. They were big and natural and Abraham wasn't allowed to cut them down. The Forest and the highway were on the other side. Looking out her bedroom window, the house could have been anywhere in town, in any town in the county.

Judy knocked, and then opened the door without waiting for a response. She was carrying a hamper full of clean laundry, and dumped it out unceremoniously onto Greta's twin bed. She'd unpinned her braids, and they swung around her shoulders.

"Thanks, Judy," Greta said. The lumps of clothes on the bed made faces: this sleeve was a mouth, that sock an eye. There were highlights of living at home: when Judy washed her clothes, they were always softer and better than Greta remembered them. Abraham's beef stew that cooked in red wine all day long and made the house smell like it was somewhere in France. Knowing that the keys to the schoolbus were hanging on a hook in the kitchen, as though anyone could take them and drive it off into the sunset. Sometimes Greta took the keys and sat in the driver's seat and pretended she was on the highway—a different highway, one that went somewhere.

"Sure, love." Judy came over with the empty hamper hiked against her hip and stood on her tippy-toes to kiss Greta's forehead. She smelled like caramelized butter and soap. They stood next to each other and stared out the window into the night, though Greta looked mostly at their reflection in the glass. The fairytales Greta had always liked most were the ones from Judy's childhood—the banker father, the homemaker mother, the tidy house in the suburbs of Long Island. Her grandfather had worn a suit every day of his adult life. He'd had a tie rack. Her grandmother wore pearls. It was almost too much to bear, the thousands of choices that led up to Greta's existence. It just all seemed so unlikely. How could you know which parking lot to sleep in, which wax to use, which tie to wear? The choices went back farther than the trees, back so far they became myth. Greta had never met her grandparents. There was something about Abraham they didn't agree with.

In August, cars pulled in and out all day long. Women had yappy little dogs on leashes and sometimes even in their purses. Two boys, older than her, but still not grown-ups, came into the ticket booth on their own.

"Want tickets for the Forest, for the Ferris wheel, or both?" Greta's pointer finger hovered over the cash register.

The boys looked at each other, which gave Greta the opportunity to do the same. The one on the left was shorter, darker. His hair was so dark brown that it was almost black, like in comic books. The sun was directly overhead, and Greta almost expected to see little illustrated windowpanes when he turned his cheek towards his friend.

The other one spoke first. He was taller and thinner. Judy would have called him a stringbean. "Uh, I don't know. Which would you recommend?" he said.

Greta stroked the tips of her wings. "I'd do both. I mean, are you in a hurry?"

They were not.

Boys from school were out of the question. If they were

interested, it invariably had more to do with wanting to get a blow job on the Ferris wheel and then tell everyone at school. It didn't matter that she hadn't done that, wouldn't do that. When people heard that you lived in an amusement park, they'd believe anything. When boys came from other places, though, it was like the opening scenes from *Grease*. No one from home was there to watch, so you could say whatever you wanted. No one would ever know how nice you'd been, how sweet. Everyone always promised to write and to call. It almost didn't matter that they never did.

The stringbean's name was Jeff; the other one was Nathan. They were from somewhere in Ohio where they had the biggest roller coasters in the country. They were driving home from a trip to New York. Stringbean thought he remembered the Forest from a trip he'd taken with his parents as a kid. They liked the Ferris wheel, and Nathan said he liked her wings.

After selling them tickets, Greta took the boys on a private tour of the property. It was the end of a slow day. If someone really needed to get in, they could buy a ticket from Judy at the restaurant. Greta left a sign.

The first stop was the other side of the old barn, where the invisible unicorns lived. "Don't bother looking," Greta said. "There aren't any." Nathan whinnied, and pawed the ground with his sneaker.

The second stop was the path up the hill. Greta knew better than to take them to the house; they didn't want to see that she really lived there. They wanted her to be a magical tree fairy, who only wore wings and flip-flops and never went to the bathroom. A few feet up the trail, the path veered to the right. Greta hopped the fence and led them to the left.

They sat in the still-roofless Hall of Mirrors, which had still yet to acquire either a hall or a mirror. They each picked a wall and leaned against it, their feet all touching in the middle. It was just starting to get dark, and overhead flocks of birds settled onto branches and told each other what was for dinner.

"So what do you do for fun around here?" The Stringbean waved his feet back and forth, sending his Converse All-Stars into Greta, then Nathan, then Greta again.

"Oh, you know, stuff. Gets pretty wild, as you can imagine," Greta said. They were maybe twenty. Greta did the math and mentally bumped herself up to eighteen. There was no reason not to. Nobody wanted to feel creepy.

There were things Greta could tell in the Forest that she couldn't at school, like which boy wanted to kiss her. The Stringbean was the chattier of the two, but Nathan looked at her in a way that she recognized, like he was trying to put together a stereo without having read the instructions. Every now and then there was a breakthrough, but mostly his brow stayed tight with concentration. He kept his eyes on Greta's mouth. She could see it, even in the dark.

"Do you get out of here much?" Nathan asked. He had small hands, almost feminine, and he rubbed them together, making a swooshing sound. "You should come to Ohio. There's all kinds of crazy stuff there."

He was handsome, but didn't really seem to know it. That was the best kind of boy, Greta knew. If they'd gone to the same school, he might still have talked to her in the halls, might still have looked at her that way. His eyes were a better brown than hers, richer. There was so much to see in the dark, if you really looked.

"Oh yeah? Like what?" Greta thought about the part in the movie where she would just decide to go somewhere, with boys she'd just met. They would stop at the same trucker diners that Abraham liked, but the food would taste completely different. Sometimes, when she was in the right mood, Judy would talk about her life before Abraham, all the places she'd been, where she'd eaten the best pieces of pie in the whole country. Greta liked to think that someday she would have those stories, too. She and Nathan would drink coffee all day long, just so they could talk more. They would wish that Ohio were farther away. Maybe when they hit Ohio they'd just keep going. Eventually Stringbean would understand, and he'd buy a bus ticket home.

"There's the Boy with the Boot. In the middle of this fountain, there's like this little boy. A statue. I don't know." Nathan shrugged. "In Cleveland, there's the world's largest rubber stamp."

Greta nodded. "What about movie theaters? Or places where the waitresses wear rollerskates?" Maybe in some states, it was still 1975, or even earlier.

Stringbean pulled a pack of cigarettes out of his pocket and they all took one. Soon the glowing red tips were the only things they could see. Greta started writing words in the air, and the boys had to guess. She wrote *Ohio*, with all those loop-de-loops. She wrote *Hello*. She wrote her name.

The Forest was closed. Greta could hear Abraham pulling down shutters and flipping switches. Nathan and the reluctant Stringbean drove to the campgrounds in the Enchanted Forest

State Park for the night, so that they could come back the next day. Everyone agreed that they hadn't gotten their money's worth.

At night, Abraham liked to drink wine and smoke a few joints. Judy valiantly tried to keep up, but her body just wasn't big enough. She had one big mug full of red wine and declared herself tippled.

"I'm going to bed!" she announced. She kissed Greta and Abraham on their foreheads and padded down the hall to the bedroom, wiggling her bottom slightly as she went, and sometimes wagging a finger. Greta thought there was probably always music playing inside her mother's head, music only she could hear.

Abraham passed his joint to Greta. The kitchen table was dark and wide, old wood. It had been a door in the barn, before the barn became the ticket booth and the Abandoned Unicorn Rehabilitation Center. Outside the window, the Forest was dark, the forest was dark, the world was dark. Only the light over the Enchanted Forest sign still lit the night, and the road at the bottom of the sloping hill.

"So," Greta said, sucking in a cloud of smoke. "Do you ever think about what would have happened if mom's bus hadn't broken down here?" Fate was an issue. The gray cloud rumbled around in her throat, drawing maps to places that might have been, places that could be.

"That bus and I," Abraham said, "have an unspoken connection. It would have found me eventually." He beckoned for the joint with a flick of his eyebrow. The coarse hairs over his upper lip somehow managed to escape being singed. The smell was warm and skunky. Greta wondered if people driving by could smell it, too.

"You know that's not what I meant." Greta's eyes felt tighter in her skull, as though they were receding further into her head. She put her palms over them to make sure they stayed put.

"Well, babygirl, some questions are beyond us all." Abraham extended his arms over his head, leaning back with the joint in his mouth. He tilted his neck so that his face was pointed toward the ceiling, and let out a smoky burp.

"You are disgusting," Greta said.

"That may be, but I am yours." Abraham rocked forward in his chair, and patted Greta's hand with his own. She wondered what it was like to have a normal-sized father, what that would be like. Would you grow up and think everything else was normal, too? Would you see yourself everywhere, in every family's station wagon? How would you remember which family you belonged to?

The next day, Nathan came back alone. Stringbean waited at the park. When Nathan came back to the ticket booth, he smiled. His teeth weren't perfect, but they were close, with only a slight snaggle along the bottom row.

"Hi," Greta said.

"Hi," Nathan said back.

He was as good as anyone. There was something safe about his face, something that she knew she wouldn't love forever. In Ohio, roller coasters pierced the sky, unapologetically reaching for something higher than the earth. As far as she was concerned, there was no going back.

It was a Monday, and the park was closed. Judy was at a day-long meditation retreat in Rhinebeck, and Abraham was being Walt at the Enchanted Forest Public Library—his one appointment of the summer season. Greta packed a small duffel bag—wings, underwear, socks—and took it with her in Nathan's car. She couldn't leave without saying goodbye.

The Library was only two rooms long, with low ceilings and brown carpeting. No one went except for people with kids and lonely old people. The old people were Abraham's biggest fans. They came every time, no matter how frequently. The back room, where Abraham did his readings, smelled like pee and mildew.

Greta and Nathan had to stand in the back; all the seats were taken. Their wrists might have touched, but they didn't hold hands. Two ladies had their plastic bonnets on; the forecast looked iffy, and it was better to be safe.

Abraham was halfway through *Song of Myself*, and it sounded like he was gearing up to do the whole thing. Greta wondered if the old people knew it was okay to take bathroom breaks.

He was unscrewing the locks from the doors. He was unscrewing the doors from their jambs. Abraham's voice bounced off the walls and the ceiling. Foamy spit would begin to form in the corners of his mouth, if it hadn't already. The halves of his cheeks not covered with hair would begin to color, peach to pink, then pink to red.

If Abraham were Walt Whitman, not just for pretend but for real, he'd write poems about the Forest, and about her, and about Judy's pies and the view from the top of the Ferris wheel and the burl creatures from California. He'd say *I sing the apple pie electric.* He'd say *But oh daughter! My daughter!* He'd say *I will live forever.* He'd say *Don't ever go.* Here was something that Greta thought about: if you had to pick the person you loved the most, who would it be? Greta thought that if someone asked Abraham that question, he would probably say her. Sure, parents were supposed to say things like that, but she thought he might even really mean it.

There were people who were just meant to get you somewhere, like Judy's old boyfriend the candlemaker. They weren't supposed to stick around. And sometimes people had to stay put. Greta thought of the Forest filled with drying candles, their wicks still connected and slung over low branches. She looked at Abraham, who was raising his hands to the sky. The room seemed bigger, somehow. There would be a better time to go.

FLY-OVER STATE

I watched the neighbor's kid from our screened-in porch. He had a BB gun—the kind of gun parents reluctantly give eleven-year-old boys on their birthdays. Of course, the kid was not eleven. The kid wasn't even a kid. He was of an indeterminate age, hovering; he could have been eighteen or thirty, with skin the pale color of sliced bread. If he hadn't been so big, we might not have noticed him at all. It appeared that none of the other neighbors did.

The boy wedged his gun against his thick shoulder, and with the orange felt of his hunting cap hanging low over his ears, he was only slightly more threatening than Elmer Fudd. He aimed at the squirrels attacking the dying hostas between our houses.

That summer was unusually harsh for Wisconsin. It was ninety degrees, and our boxes were still on the porch. The BB boy's mother came over with a pitcher of iced tea. "Well, hello there," she said, pulling open the screen door. "Looks like you've got your work cut out for you!"

The pitcher sweated as much as I did, and dropped little streams of water onto the warped wooden planks of the porch.

I took it out of her hands and set it down on our coffee table, which was on the porch next to our dining room chairs. I motioned for her to sit.

"I'm Margaret, from next door." She pointed, as if I hadn't seen her walk out of her house and up my steps. She kept a beautiful garden, which was seemingly unharmed by the heat. I suspected she had a secret watering technique, a magic potion made of horse manure and sunshine. In New York, I had worked hard to cultivate a small cactus plant on our fire escape overlooking Prospect Park West, a gift from a friend who belonged to the Food Co-Op who'd said that it could withstand anything, even me. The plant was dead in three months. I considered it a success.

From what I could tell, the neighbor's house was the mirror image of ours—our dining room faced their dining room, our bedroom their bedroom. They had curtains, however. Watching us must have been like watching reality television, unedited and endless. Live! Moving! People! It had taken us weeks to buy any sort of window covering, and even then, they were shower curtains. They kept out the light, and if it was raining, it didn't matter if we closed the windows. Of course, it didn't rain. Still, I thought, terribly clever.

"Sophie," I said, shaking her hand. "From the porch."

"Where are you all from?" Margaret sounded like she was from the South, or at least she had been some years ago.

"We moved from New York, but originally I'm from Connecticut, and my husband is from Philadelphia. So, East Coast, I guess. We're from the East Coast."

"Mmm," Margaret said, as though eating something

delicious. The full pitcher of iced tea sat untouched between us.

"I think I know where the glasses are," I said, getting up. "Can I get you a glass?"

Margaret looked longingly at her house like a blind mole searching for its dinner, and was on the verge of protesting as I pried open the first box.

Only a few days before the move to Wisconsin, James caught me in bed with the laptop, emailing building managers in Los Angeles about cozy cottages up by Griffith Park. Ample room for four-legged friends! We could find a dog en route—surely there were a thousand ASPCAs between New York and California. Not one of those Hollywood dogs that can fit in your purse; we'd get something big, something like Marmaduke, a dog with jowls and gallons of drool. Shopping for new apartments was like shopping for new lives, an easier fix than dieting or yoga. I could garden, and he could hammer together bookshelves in the garage. He would become an apprentice at a motorcycle shop and we would get tattoos that said Forever. Forever Sophie. Or maybe something dramatic: Sophie's Choice. People who didn't know him would ask him about it in restaurants—James would wear tank-tops to show it off, along with all the others: the red-scaled koi fish, the winking mermaid. You must really like Meryl Streep, they'd say. James would take a sip of coffee—or no, bourbon, even in the morning—and laugh. No, he'd say, I really like her, and nod his chin towards me. The other patrons would look at me, and through all the gleaming silver rods and balls sticking out of my nose and ears and eyebrows, they would think that I was beautiful.

Of course, James had no tattoos, no metal objects poking out of his face. He was an academic, the kind of man who had always enjoyed spending his Saturday afternoons in dreary library carrels. We'd come to Wisconsin because he'd gotten a job at a local college, although not the University, which was what people always asked.

He taught two courses in the English department, both of which were supposed to introduce the students to some names they'd heard only as movie tie-ins: Austen and Dickens and Eliot. James had written his dissertation about the role of gossip in *Emma* and *Middlemarch*. A few years in, when he'd started bringing home the glossy tabloids, I'd thought it was some brilliant research, just the ticket. Then he started saying things to me like, "Can you believe they're getting a divorce? I really thought if anyone had a chance, it would be them." He would shake his head and have to go to bed early, his thin chest sunken with disappointment. The novels seemed beside the point, unable to rescue him from the harsh facts of the day.

It seemed inevitable that we would spend our lives going from college town to college town, always having the same conversations about departmental politics and the weather. One merely had to adjust to the scale of possible adventures. Red Lobster had an All-You-Can-Eat Lobster Tail dinner once a week; the aisles of Home Depot were satisfyingly endless. There were still small excitements in the world, things our friends in New York couldn't even imagine.

A few weeks in, we got invited over to another professor's house for dinner. They lived on the other side of town, the side with all the trees and expensive shops. 'The Professor and his wife,' as a phrase, always bothered me. I refused to let James introduce me as his wife—he had to say my name first, then wife. The order was important; it was easy for people to get the wrong impression.

The conversation at dinner was standard, almost as standard as the food. "I just love salmon," I told the Professor's wife, whose name I couldn't remember because she'd been introduced as Wife First, Name Second. "Really love it." The men talked about department politics. James was nodding at everything the Professor said, making mental notes about who was overly flirtatious with his students, who hid what in his desk drawers.

They had a large dining room, with plates and glasses that all matched. I kicked James under the table. The Professor sat to my left, at the head of the table. His wife sat facing me, placidly smiling.

"So, Sophie," she said. "What do you plan to do here, while James is off molding young minds?" She tented her fingers in front of her, as though holding one of the young minds in her hands.

"Well, you can remove mold with any sharp knife," I said. "Then you can just go ahead and eat it."

"Excuse me?" She was still smiling, but James had returned my kick.

"I'm thinking about culinary school," I said. "I hear there's an excellent schnitzel academy just down the road. Or was it the wurst one, James, do you remember?"

James daubed his mouth with the corner of his napkin, pretending to be civilized. He looked at the Professor's wife. "Sophie works freelance. She's just published an article in one of the local New York papers."

The wife nodded. "You know," she said, "if you're looking for some good schnitzel, I know just where you should go." She looked to her husband and widened her eyes, as though remembering a particularly impressive sausage.

I excused myself and went to pee, happy to have a moment alone, a moment with only the belongings of strangers and not the strangers themselves. I sat down and was surprised to find myself staring at a familiar panel of fabric. "We have the same curtains," I cried. "Only ours are in the bedroom!" The Professor's wife materialized on the other side of the bathroom door. I could see the shadows of her chunky shoes moving back and forth across the small pane of light coming from the kitchen. After washing my hands, I stood for a minute in front of the curtains, and asked them which they preferred, seeing the outside world, or seeing nothing but tiles, shampoo bottles, and nudity.

There had been other jobs, other interviews. James brought two suits to the rounds of interviews at the hotel in midtown, one pinstriped, one gray, and he'd changed in the bathroom in between. He thought the pinstriped made him look like a businessman, and was better for the larger schools. The gray suit, he thought, made him look like a real intellectual. We could have gone anywhere, that's what we'd decided. Tucson.

Miami. Detroit. Each time James presented me with a city, I'd walk to the bookstore on Seventh Avenue and sit down in the travel section. I'd find us a neighborhood, a coffee shop to frequent. I knew where we'd go for fun, to people-watch. There were the restaurants our parents would take us when they came to visit; first mine, then his. There was the park I could take walks in, and the places we could meet for lunch during the school day. The suits would take us there. I never imagined we'd actually leave New York. I had a part-time job, and friends, and neighbors whose names I didn't know. We were settled. There were never any boxes in my daydreams.

When I finally told my mother the truth about where we were going, she gasped and said, "A fly-over state?"

My mother had lived in Greenwich, Connecticut, for fifty of her sixty-five years. The intervening years—college in neighboring Massachusetts, an early marriage in California— were looked upon as a sad experiment, the kind where the potion turns purple instead of orange and hisses briefly, instead of bubbling dramatically to the top of the beaker.

"It's not so bad, Mom." We were on the telephone, and I could tell from the static on her end that she was outside in the yard. There would be someone gardening nearby; she was supervising.

"Mm hmm, sure, sure." I could see the mounds of dirt, her careful steps. "Sophie, my dear, you know I support whatever it is you want to do. I just want you to be happy. Really. Now, who did you say was subletting the place in the city? You know, the weather has just been lovely. Just lovely."

I placed a finger down the front of my tank-top and

swiped at the sweat that had begun to pool between my breasts. "Yes, mother, I believe you already said that." Surely the public pools in Wisconsin bore little resemblance to their inner-city counterparts. I closed my eyes and imagined myself submerged in a swimming pool the size of Home Depot, with rooms to paddle in and out of.

Margaret had a tight mouth, small features and the personality to match, but she was in charge of the neighborhood committee, so she extended an invitation to the annual gathering at our mutual neighbor's house across the street. They'd invited over the local policeman and a firefighter and all the dogs and children. It was an event.

The Nelsons—their name was on the mailbox—were a tall, blond family with two golden retrievers. They liked to throw sticks, which seemed to be a major hobby in the neighborhood. James and I rang the doorbell at six, as directed.

A woman with red suspenders and Wellies opened the door. The firefighter. "You must be John and Susan," she said, "from the pink house across the street."

"I always thought it was more of a dusty rose than a proper pink," I said, "but maybe you're talking about some other house, with some other people. I'm Sophie, and this is James. Maybe we're in the wrong place. Is this one of those keys-in-the-bowl parties?"

The firelady waved her hand in front of her face. "Oh, no, that's right. James and Sophie. It's hard to keep track, such turnover. You planning on staying long?" She was eating a large, flat cookie the color of cardboard, and when she took a bite, a cloud of dust settled on her black T-shirt. "No offense."

"None taken," James said. "Always a pleasure to meet one of the city's bravest." I hadn't even noticed that the firelady was pretty, but she was. She had curly, dyed-red hair, and crumbs all over her bottom lip, which was rather pouty and plump. The suspenders interacted poorly with her breasts, which were also rather plump. I wanted to remind James that we were no longer living in a city of eight million, and that you probably didn't have to be all that brave to rescue cats from trees and save college kids from mishaps with their barbeques, but instead I excused myself and went to find the cookies. I made a mental note to call friends at home and tell them about our yard: it existed. They could come over and we could stand in it, eating cookies, even if we were too afraid to commit to buying lawn furniture.

The Nelsons had framed photos on every available surface. They enjoyed skiing in the winter, sailing in the summer, and smiling all year round. Even the teenagers were pimple-free and well-adjusted. I nodded a hello to all the ladies with sensible haircuts who were gathered in the living room, and pushed through the swinging door towards what I hoped would be the kitchen.

A thick-bodied wall of a teenaged boy sat on one of the stools, facing the back window. I recognized him from the yard. Margaret's over-sized son. The Nelsons lived on the better side of the street, the lake side, and their kitchen windows overlooked the water. Outside, people sped by on small boats, laughing. The athletes—the ones with the bulging arms and the spandex unitards—steered kayaks and canoes. It made me tired just to watch.

"Hi, I'm your next-door neighbor," I said.

The boy grunted. He was wearing his orange hunting cap, which I realized I had never seen him without, despite the oppressive heat. He spun around on the stool and faced me. "I'm Mud," he seemed to say. He looked less like a teenager from the front. His jaw was too wide, his forehead too big.

He'd said either 'Mud' or 'Mutt,' both of which I was fairly sure were not names that nice people gave to their children. "I've met your mother," I said. "She brought us some iced tea, my husband and I."

"Whoop-de-doo," Mud said, spinning back around.

"Know where the cookies are?" I was actually enjoying this, the first sign of unfriendliness in a month.

"In the living room, with all the freaks," he said. "But they're probably poison. The Nelsons eat babies. I've seen them. They used to have like twelve kids, you know."

"Poison, huh? I'll take my chances."

He raised and lowered his hunting cap, as if saluting the happy people scooting by on motorboats, and mumbled something about karate.

Back in the living room, the firelady had moved on to the bald guy from three doors down. James had acquired a mug full of alcoholic cider. The whole room smelled like nutmeg: Christmas in August.

"I think the boy who lives next door is a serial killer," I whispered.

James nodded. "Good cider," he said, unimpressed by my discovery.

Mrs. Nelson and the local policeman appeared in front of us. "Jim, Sally, this is Officer Sheffield. He's been in charge of our little neighborhood for, oh, how long is it now, Greg, ten years?"

Officer Sheffield nodded. "And not a B & E since. One stolen car, and even that turned out to be a mistake. City towed it around the corner. Mrs. Dearborn never did leave the house too much."

"Murder? Rape? Animal cruelty?" I said, thinking of everything my mother warned me about when we moved to Brooklyn. Mud had been of age for at least a few years, and I couldn't imagine there wasn't a pile of missing cats somewhere.

Mrs. Nelson clasped a fist over her sternum. "Oh, gosh, no! Where did you think you'd moved, Milwaukee?" Her cheeks had darts of crimson in them. "Course, you probably won't be here long. That pink house is just a revolving door, honestly."

"It's a rental," I said, realizing when I said it that our house was the only rental on the block. Maybe something unseemly had happened there: adultery, Judaism, modern dance.

Behind them, Mud skulked out of the kitchen and towards the plate of cookies on the mantelpiece. He took three, and returned to the kitchen before the announcements began. There was going to be a potluck over the holidays, and not everyone could bring dessert. There were audible sighs.

James and I held hands as we crossed the street and walked back to our house. "Don't you think," I asked, "that if that party had been in New York, the cookies would have been an ironic stroke of genius?"

He nodded, and pulled a folded napkin out of his jacket

pocket, sending crumbs to the sidewalk in front of our steps. "Unironic cookies taste better." He opened the napkin and showed me a short stack of pilfered baked goods.

There'd been some kind of run-in with a telephone pole over on the south side of town, and Mud's car was totaled. I'd seen him roar up and down the (one-way, dead-end) street, and wasn't surprised to hear the news. I was surprised, however, to hear it from Mud himself. James was at school, and I was alone at home, ostensibly looking for a job, which meant that I was spending all day in my pajamas watching daytime television. Not that there weren't opportunities open to me. Craigslist thought that I should be a shot girl at a bar. I could spend my evenings pouring Jagermeister down the throats of eighteen-year-olds while wearing a whistle. I could work at the mall by the airport, twisting strips of dough into pretzels, or photograph crying babies for Christmas cards. James thought I should join a book club, you know, to meet some people. The only book clubs I found were for lonely lesbians and at-risk youths. Maybe I could cut my hair. The doorbell surprised me.

"Hey." Mud was wearing his orange cap. Something in his pocket seemed to be moving, and it took me a few seconds to realize it was his hand, jiggling around some loose change. "Can I have a ride?"

"Now?" I was wearing pajama bottoms patterned with flying pigs and a faded T-shirt. "Where?"

Mud nodded. "Got to get to work." He paused. "Nice pigs. I used to be able to fly, too, before my mom went all psycho on me and cut off my wings. You see the X-Men movie?" He kicked the porch hard with the toe of his sneaker.

"I'll change. Just give me a minute, okay?"

James and I had seen Mud at work—he bagged groceries and stocked shelves at the giant grocery store on the outskirts of town, out by where all the chain restaurants went to procreate. He usually added the store's logo baseball cap over his own, which made his ears look like they were made of orange felt.

When we were about halfway to the grocery store, Mud cleared his throat. "I need to make a stop first. Pull over up there?"

He motioned towards a small strip mall on the side of the four-lane road. It housed a Thai restaurant, a decaying ballroom dance studio, and a place called The Pleasure Emporium. It was after lunchtime, nearly three o'clock. I could guess where Mud needed to go. I pulled into an open space in front of the restaurant and put the car in park. "Hurry up," I said.

He looked almost beautiful with relief. Mud's face was round and lumpy, full of hydrogenated oils. He was at least eighteen, that much I knew, and so, really, who was I to stop him. It took him three minutes to get back in the car, with a small brown paper package in hand. Lucky he works at the grocery store, I thought, otherwise the bag would have looked awfully suspicious.

"If you open that bag in my car," I said, but chose not to finish my sentence. I turned back onto the highway. The car groaned as I accelerated. It was getting colder.

James and I ate dinner on the porch, using fold-out TV trays, our laps kept warm by two woolen blankets, gifts from James's mother. She'd heard the word 'Wisconsin' and immediately sprung into action, sending boxes of down-filled winter apparel and frozen red meat. We liked to watch the neighbors scuttle past, their dogs pulling the arms out of their sockets. Sometimes they would wave and try a stab at our names, but most often they'd just grab a stick and throw it farther down the sidewalk.

In lieu of buying a replacement automobile, Mud had taken to using his mother's bicycle. The bike was pink and white and had a large basket hanging off its handlebars, in which Mud placed six-packs of beer and other important objects from the outside world. We'd see him ride to and fro, his round cheeks always flushed with the cold, his orange ear flaps flopping against the wind. He looked altogether too heavy for the bike to support; I was waiting for the day the metal frame would collapse beneath him like a soda can.

"A boy just can't ride a bicycle," James said. "He's never going to get a girlfriend."

"He lives in his mother's basement and bags groceries," I said, "I don't think the bike is his problem."

James took a sip of wine. Like most things, it was cheaper in Wisconsin, and we'd bought too much, as though we had friends to help us drink it. James was on red, and I was on white. We were having a race.

"And anyway, lots of glamorous people ride bikes. Think about Audrey Hepburn—a born bicyclist." I pictured Mud in capri pants and ballet flats, plucking a ukulele on his fire escape, a handkerchief knotted over the crown of his hunting cap. A ukulele would fit in his basket, for sure.

"Einstein rode a bicycle." James opened his mouth wide and packed in a mouthful of mashed potatoes. Someone—a second cousin, or a first cousin once-removed, we were never sure— had given us an electric potato masher for our wedding, and the dish had become one of his specialties. "But," he said, his fork in the air, "Einstein was a genius."

Across the street, a handful of Nelsons erupted in a cheer. One of them, a boy of about twelve, was wearing a football uniform, complete with helmet and shoulder pads.

"Look," I said, "The Incredible Hulk."

James examined the mound of beaten potatoes on his fork. "Do you think that the water here contains more nutrients? You know, like the water in New York makes better bagels?"

"Yes," I said. "I think they're trying to build a better man. Isn't Paul Bunyan from Wisconsin? Maybe that's what they're going for." I drank the rest of my wine and peered up into the empty glass.

"Imagine the sticks they'd need to throw for an ox."

I reached over and pulled James's head closer to mine and gave him a kiss. He had the cheekbones of a movie star, sharp enough to maim.

Mrs. and Mr. Mud were retired. Mr. Mud was an elusive creature and seemed to leave the house even less than I did, which was saying a lot. He was tall and thick, like his son, with silvery hair that caught the sun like in a shampoo commercial. Margaret had worked in real estate, selling houses like ours to people like her. They had two flags in front of their house, Irish and American. Sometimes Mr. Mud would rake the leaves, but mostly that was Mud's job. I was surprised his mother trusted him around her flower beds with a weapon as dangerous as an aged, rusty rake.

Behind their house, next to the garage, the Muds had a tool shed, which I had always thought was a metaphoric term for the drawer in the kitchen with the screwdriver and the tape measure. I couldn't believe anyone had enough square feet, let alone acreage. Most days, Mud would spend a few hours walking around the house with his BB gun, but sometimes just with a big stick that he'd poke the ground with, as though he were looking for intruders hiding in the grass. Every now and then he'd raise the gun or the stick to his shoulder and take aim at an invisible enemy, or a particularly brash chipmunk. He would mouth the word 'pow,' even if he wasn't going to pull the trigger.

I looked out the open window in the kitchen and watched Mud rake up a few dozen leaves that had gathered behind the house. He then set the rake down on the driveway and pulled out a pack of cigarettes and a lighter. I thought for a moment that he was going to set the leaves on fire, but instead he just lit up a smoke, leaned back against the tool shed, and shut his eyes. It was a warm day, and the orange cap was set back on his head, leaving room for some air to circulate. It took a moment for the smell of the smoke to snake under my open window, and another moment for me to realize what he was smoking was not, in fact, a cigarette. I went outside.

Mud started to look a little flustered as I approached. "Hey, it's cool," I said, "Can I take a hit?"

He blew out the lungful of smoke and coughed. "You're

weird," he said. "You're like this totally weird lady next door."

"Same to you," I said. "Cheers." I took a hit of the joint and held it.

"I'm not a lady," Mud said. "I'm a Mud."

"An excellent point." Around our feet, the collected leaves were being blown about by the wind. Mud and I watched as they scattered around the yard, crackling. Mud already looked stoned. Under the raised brim of his cap, his small eyes seemed to have receded into his skull.

"How long have you worked at the grocery store?" I asked.

"Since I was sixteen. Back then it was just on the weekends."

"And how long ago was that?" I tried to guess.

Mud held up his fingers and counted. His nails were short and clean. "Eight years, on and off."

Mud was only seven years younger than I was; he didn't look twenty-four. "That's a lot of groceries," I said.

"No shit." He stepped on some leaves, making a good dry noise that reminded me of fall. "What kind of name is Sophie?" he asked. "It sounds like a cat or something."

I shrugged. "It was my grandmother's name. What kind of name is Mud?"

"You think my name is Mud?"

I wasn't sure if he was joking. His potato face was blank, with no hint of a stoned smile. "Yes." I said. "Yes, I do."

Mud nodded, and said, "It's cool, right."

"Right." He had asked me a question, and I had given the correct answer. He looked pleased. I wondered what other names had come and gone. Snake. Hot Rod. Lucky.

The closest coffee shop was hiring—they stuck an index card on the door saying so. I'd poured coffee in high school, and I figured it might be a good reason to get out of the house, especially now that it was getting cold and there was nothing else to do that didn't involve snowshoes. Counter Culture sold six different blends, all with names that were supposed to be political puns. Jessie, the girl who hired me, had defected from her graduate studies at the University. She had blonde dreadlocks and emitted the faint scent of spoiled coconut. She told me that she'd found a new path, and that the path was coffee. "I just want to make people happy," she said.

"I just want to get out of the house," I said.

Jessie, sweetly, put her hand on my shoulder. "Know how to make foam?"

Sometimes James would come in and grade papers in one of the threadbare armchairs by the window. He liked to drink the Dark Web of Lies Colombian Roast. Of course, he poured in two solid glugs of milk, making it more of a Partially Cloudy Web of Lies. Jessie measured everything in glugs. I was learning.

"You know," he said one afternoon, "if everything goes well here this semester, I could probably apply for the assistant professor job in Milwaukee. We'd barely have to move. Wouldn't that be great?" James was wearing his reading glasses, and looked studious, which was the only look available. He was too thin to be anything but an academic. When we were in college and I first saw him naked, he reminded me of those ads they used to have in the back of Archie comics, where the skinny guy gets sand kicked in his face. Ectomorph. Concave.

I'd gone on a diet immediately, so as not to crush him.

"Milwaukee? Isn't that where they have all the rapes and animal cruelty?" In Milwaukee, we could live by an even bigger lake, in a house with even more rooms. As it was, there was too much space. My laptop and I shared a room that James generously referred to as "my office," which by virtue of its existence exerted so much pressure over us that we had to avoid it and stay in the kitchen.

"Honey, would you mind?" James offered up his empty mug.

On Saturdays, James made pancakes and I would do interpretative dance, miming the cracking of the eggs, the stirring of the batter. If he was feeling particularly good, James would rummage through the cupboard for his mortar and pestle and then grind some cinnamon sticks and vanilla beans. He'd found the recipe in a magazine, ascribed to an actress who hadn't eaten carbohydrates in a decade. We took her word for it. I was just reaching the climax of my movement, wherein the flour and liquid have emulsified, with my arms raised overheard, when the doorbell rang. It was nine-fifteen in the morning. James and I walked together towards the front door, he carrying the bowl of batter.

Mud stood with his back to the door, as though he'd rung the bell accidentally, and was waiting for a bus to stop, just there, on our porch.

"Can I help you?" James gave the batter a flick. He wasn't wearing his glasses, and squinted into the light.

Mud turned, surprised to hear a man's voice. He looked at

me over James's shoulder. "Same deal as last time."

I hadn't told James about driving Mud to work. After all, he no longer told me the minutiae of his days, the way he had when he'd first started teaching, when I'd known all the students' names and their brief, young resumés. I was only being neighborly. Charitable. It would have been like telling James every time I gave a dollar to the Cerebral Palsy Fund in those round metal jars at the movies, or cooed at someone's less than handsome baby.

"Sorry, Mud, we're in the middle of making breakfast." I scooted in front of James, blocking the doorway with my arm.

Beneath the orange hat, Mud's face began to glow slightly pink, like skin after a punch. He nodded, turned away, and trudged slowly down the steps and back towards his house.

"Penny drive at school," I said to James as I shut the door, pushing his back towards the kitchen. "Like UNICEF, you know? For Sudanese refugee camps, I think." I shook my head, saying, it's nothing. I wasn't sure why I was lying to him.

"He's still in school?" James put the bowl of batter down on the counter beside the stove, and stuck a finger in the pale, milky goo.

"Community college, I think." I tried to think of a single thing Mud might be interested in enough to continue his studies. Auto repair, maybe. Accessory design.

"Huh." James turned the knob for one of the back burners. We listened to the slow clicking of the igniter, watching for the short blue flames to appear.

Margaret came around one night with flyers. In addition to her work with the neighborhood committee, she also volunteered at the Eastside Senior Center, which occupied two small buildings across the narrow river near our house. Some of the members were putting on a show, an abbreviated production of *Guys and Dolls,* which turned out to mean a handful of scenes that could all use the same props and backdrop. James had to stay late at work, as it was nearly midterms, and so I went alone and stood in the back. Rows of folding chairs were set up in what looked like a dining hall, with a small wooden platform at the back of the room. The overhead lights were dimmed, but there was still enough light that the residents with canes could see what they were about to trip over.

Three of the Nelson kids were working at the makeshift concession stand, where a slice of chocolate cake was a dollar and glasses of milk were free. Margaret, I understood from seeing her flit about with a plastic baggie full of safety pins and a feather boa draped around her neck, was doing costumes, which made me like her more.

A seventy-three-year-old woman wearing a nightie got up on stage. She had the lithe legs of a former dancer, and even though her voice was shaky, I knew by the way the men in the audience held their hands over their heads to clap that she was a hit before she sang a note. Margaret had painted the woman's lips magenta, so even from the back of the room, I could see her mouth open and close. In the city, she would have been a thirty-year-old guy in drag, legs and chest waxed, fake eyelashes and wrinkles. If I'd had a friend next to me, I would have squeezed her arm and said can you believe this—but kitsch wasn't kitsch if you were alone. I could hardly hear the woman's voice, but I knew all the words to the song, and mouthed along with her. My grandmother Sophie had lived in a place like this, and all I remembered were the hallways full of people who'd suddenly found themselves single after fifty years. They'd had a little chapel on the ground floor, wheelchair accessible, and they had lots of weddings. No one's family ever understood. If I died, I wanted James to get married again as soon as possible, either to a librarian or a reporter for a trashy magazine. It was something we'd discussed.

After the performance, I found Margaret standing by the side of the stage, her cheeks flushed with success. She was folding clothes and neatly putting her little baggies back into a rolling suitcase. She'd given herself a swipe of the bright lipstick, and her thin lips seemed to hover a few inches in front of her face.

"Oh! Sophie!" She was surprised to see me, and opened a plastic wallet of baby wipes and quickly doused her face, removing all but a pinkish smudge on her chin.

"I thought it was just wonderful, Margaret, thanks for inviting me. La grippe, la grippe, la post nasal drip..." I sang a few bars to prove that I'd been paying attention. Sometimes James asked me to sing to him while he mashed the potatoes, the shrillness of your voice makes it go faster, he'd say, whirring away. The electric masher and I competed for volume in the kitchen, which was big enough to have a slight echo. One of these days we'd have to buy some more furniture. Maybe in Milwaukee. Maybe in Boise. Maybe in the Yukon.

Her face relaxed, which made her look both older and prettier. Mud didn't look anything like her, except for a little bit around the eyes. They both always wanted to look away. "That's very nice of you to say." She paused, and looked at me the way a girl in a clothing store would, before inaccurately overestimating your size, or, worse, getting you the correct size, which you'd rather not be. "Mud has told me that you've been very friendly to him."

I was surprised to hear that Mud spoke to his mother in full sentences, that he knew the word 'friendly.' "Your son is an interesting individual," I said. Clowns were interesting. People on death row were interesting. Mud qualified.

She lowered her gaze and nodded, smiling to herself. A feather from the boa around her neck disengaged itself, and we watched it fall to the floor in slow swoops.

At first, the siren sounded like a passing ambulance, just a vehicle in a hurry. The ringing continued, though, and when I looked out the bedroom window, the backyard seemed lit for a movie set, as though it were night, but with hidden flood lights illuminating each blade of grass, each shuddering leaf. The bed was empty—it was Thursday, a teaching day, and James had been gone for hours. If we'd stayed in New York, it would have been a real movie set. Once James came home, we would have gone outside and seen who the stars were, where their trailers were parked, what the craft service table had laid out for the crew. But it wasn't a set; the sky was really that yellow. The wind picked up, and whistled through the branches, sending dying leaves to the ground outside my window.

Dorothy came to mind, Kansas in black and white. One was supposed to stand in a doorway, under furniture, in the basement. I put on my slippers and walked over to the kitchen. It was the twilight zone on the other side of the house, too. But there was a light in the basement next door.

Mud didn't look as surprised as I thought he might when I knocked. Maybe he thought I needed to borrow his bicycle to go stock up on bottled water and batteries, cans of soup, whatever it is one is supposed to have on hand in case of an emergency.

"Can I come in?" The tornado siren kept howling. Where were the speakers? It was like going to a concert and sitting on one side, next to the amplifier. Everything skewed towards distortion.

In answer, Mud started walking back down the stairs. I ducked in quickly behind him before the door closed. I hoped his mother wasn't watching. Across the street, the Nelsons were probably performing search and rescue missions for all the neighborhood cats.

The basement looked like what it was, a refuge. There weren't the posters I expected, or the level of filth. A television was on, pointing the other direction. There was a pizza box, and some empty beer bottles, but mostly the space was clean. It even smelled good.

"Do you vacuum?" I asked.

Mud looked offended. "Don't you?"

"Not really. I think my husband does, sometimes, yeah, but no, I don't. Honestly, I don't really clean the house that much."

Something started to tap against the window, ting ting, like a tiny bell.

"Well, I guess that's the hail." Mud looked at my feet. I still had on my worn, terry-cloth slippers. "Those waterproof?"

The basement was one large room—he must have had to go up into the house to use the kitchen, although there was a mini-fridge, the kind kids have in their dorm rooms. It was like a loft in Tribeca, only with wall-to-wall carpet and no windows. It was practically cosmopolitan. There were even books. I stooped to look at the spines. Wedged in between the bird field guides and almanacs were novels, novels James taught, novels I hadn't read.

"You going to move?" Mud said. I shifted my body out of the way, although it didn't appear that I was blocking anything. "No," Mud shook his head. "I mean out of town."

"Maybe," I said. "I guess it depends on my husband."

"You don't have a real job?"

"Do you?" I asked.

Mud crossed his arms over his chest. He looked like the bouncer at the kind of nightclub that's well stocked with pasties and spangled G-strings. I exhaled. "I think I'm still working on that."

"So, you're from New York?"

I nodded.

"What was it like?" Mud walked behind me, and ran his finger across his rows of books. "Was it like in the movies?"

I didn't know how to tell him that nothing was as much like the movies as the last month of my life, when strange women brought me lemonade and baked goods, which I then consumed without worry that I was being poisoned for the lease to my Co-Op; that this street, where he had lived his entire life, was more beautiful than anywhere I'd ever been able to afford; that the only extreme weather that mattered in New York was when the air-conditioning went out on the subway. That it was just a place, like any other place, where people lived.

The TV flashed a blue square on the wall behind Mud's bed. Even before I walked around to see what was on, I knew what I would find there. Two enormous, saline-filled breasts bounced inches away from the camera, as someone rocked her hips back and forth somewhere below the sight line. I turned away before the director decided to change the angle.

"Do you mind?" I said.

Mud shrugged. I crossed my arms over my chest, as though it would make either of us forget that I had breasts, too. But Mud seemed neither bothered or embarrassed by my request. He lumbered over next to me, picked up the remote, and shut off the television.

"It's not a big deal," Mud said, and he was right. The actors had jobs, just like he did, just like James. They had a schedule and health insurance. They called their mothers when they remembered to do so. I thought about my mother standing on her back porch, surveying the rhododendrons. We all had to fill our days.

We took turns standing at the top of the stairs, staring out the glass pane of the window, waiting for the rain to stop, watching the fat drops of water hit my house, the trees, the shed. A puddle grew on my driveway. Across the street, my telephone might have been ringing. James could have walked by a window at school, seen the deluge, and thought to check up on me. I wondered what he'd have thought if he'd known where I was. There was gossip and there was slander; it would have been too much. When he came home, I would tell him I'd ridden out the storm in the bathtub, alone.

Mud aimed his rifle at the squirrel that had just shimmied up the tree in my yard—one of the biggest trees on the whole street. The squirrel had discovered an apple core that Mud had conveniently left sitting in the grass, alongside a handful of salted nuts, mostly cashews and almonds. Hunters, he told me, knew how to use good bait. I stood over his right shoulder, careful to stay out of the way, should the gun kick back. His extra gun lay flat against my shoulder.

"Do you ever think about moving out, you know, out of your parents' house?" I ate a small handful of nuts with my free hand, chewing them as quietly as possible so as not to disturb our quarry.

He spoke without turning around. "Not really. I like it here. I have the whole basement."

I nodded, even though he couldn't see me, and tucked my hair behind my ears. Mud told me that when it got really cold, he'd tell me where to get a good hat.

A car turned down our block—it was my car—James was home early. He pulled into our narrow garage, which was a lighter shade of pink than the house. I heard the engine rumble off. The world was overwhelmingly quiet; even the squirrel in the tree stopped nibbling and scratching.

James would want to know what I was doing, crouching in the yard with Mud, my feet straddling the remains of a flowerbed, a borrowed BB gun snug in my armpit, when I was supposed to be at work. I would have to explain it to him. I could just tell him; my path was not about coffee, or gossip. It was about something else—real estate, maybe. Standing there, waiting for my husband to emerge from the garage, I thought about how each time you moved, you left behind more and more: the antique furniture, the soft, faded T-shirts, the garbage and then the garbage cans themselves, until maybe one day you were left with only what you could carry on your back, and what was packed inside your own skin. The abandoned addresses would line up on the front lawn, and, knowing you wouldn't miss them, turn their backs as you drove away. Now that we'd left New York, we were already floating in space, tethered only to each other.

When James stepped out from the garage, his body no wider than a sapling, I raised the butt of the gun to my shoulder and peered through the sight.

"Sophie?" He said, his voice lilting up, as though unsure if it was really me. He held his briefcase in front of his body, a paper-filled bullet-proof vest. "What are you doing out here?"

"Pow," I said, smiling.

James took a few steps closer, until only a single row of dead plants lay between us. "Sophie, would you come inside with me?" James asked quietly. This was a key to public negotiation: we'd seen so many couples have it out on the sidewalk, stumbling out of nightclubs. Remaining calm in the face of uncertainty could prevent almost any disaster.

Mud chuckled.

"Shut up," I said, and he did.

In one motion, I snapped the barrel of the gun back towards the sky. Over our heads, clouds scurried out of the way. James stepped aside, into a dead rosebush the house's previous inhabitants had killed before we were even given the chance. I crossed in front of him, brushing the hair across my forehead with my free hand as I might before a job interview, making sure I looked my best. Behind me, I heard Mud start to say something about the gun I was still holding, and then he stopped himself abruptly, as if he thought I might need it, wherever I was going.

OTHER PEOPLE WE MARRIED

The advertisement had been gloriously distorted. What did it say, *3 bed/2 ba cottage on the water, w/boat slip and dock, private beach. Great for families,* was that it? It was like something Edward Gorey might have drawn, with a little girl skipping to her death. The thing barely held Bobby and his fire truck, and he was only three. *Great for families looking to off each other in the peace and quiet of the Vineyard,* is what it should have said. Jim would have put his foot down, always eager for his creature comforts. Franny just wanted to get out of the city, go somewhere with a beach. She still thought she was a cow with her leftover baby weight and yet insisted on wearing those stupid pigtails all young mothers seem to think it's their right to wear, as if they were all waiting, *gasping,* praying for someone to say, Oh, you! You can't be the mother of this child! You couldn't possibly be old enough! Charles was just along for the ride, the fourth wheel—Bobby might have been small, but he was family, and Charles was something extra.

Jim drove the Saab. It was little and black and frankly impractical for someone with limbs as long as his, but it was his car, and he loved it. He'd fold himself into the front seat like a Chinese acrobat and then wait for everyone else to climb in—Charles in front and Franny in back with the baby. Bobby had a booster seat that he was strapped into, the kind of thing that made most kids wail and squirm, but he sat there quietly eating his Cheerios, always listening to his mother when she pointed out things we passed on the highway: horses, fire trucks, hamburger stands.

Franny'd found the ad. *The New York Review of Books* ran pages of classifieds; its back pages were always filled with idyllic retreats somewhere or other, and, more often than not, a handsome older gentleman to share them with you. She sometimes cut out those for Charles, too—she'd crack up reading them aloud.

"Listen to this one, Charlie, he's perfect for you. *Long baths and foot-rubs. Looking for someone to enjoy my impressive wine cellar and library. M4M.* Impressive wine cellar, do you think that means no twist-offs? Or maybe that's what he's looking for, some good twist-offs, what do you think?" It was unclear whether Jim ever got to weigh in on whether Charles came along on their family vacations. It was doubtful. Jim was her husband, but Charles was her man, and if Franny wanted him along, well, then, he was going.

Martha's Vineyard was always a nightmare to get to, and Franny, despite her formidable organizational skills, never seemed to quite time things right. That year they showed up three minutes before the last ferry, instead of half an hour before the one they were booked on, which had departed hours earlier. Luckily, Franny was great with uniformed personnel. Jim and Charles stood by the car with their arms crossed, Bobby crouching between their shins with his fire truck. The three of them watched Fran reason with the ferry ticket boy. He was about eighteen, covered in pimples, and didn't have a shot in hell. His supervisor, maybe all of twenty, lasted about a minute, made her laugh three times, and their passage was secured. It was already dark outside when they got to the island, and Bobby snored quietly in the backseat, now in his mother's arms. Jim said the directions were bad, and it was too dark to read them, anyway, and this couldn't be where we were going.

The cottage would have been more aptly described as a shack. It was sharp around the edges and saggy in the middle, the kind of place that kids briefly sleep in before getting slashed to death by homicidal maniacs in horror movies.

"Franny, what's the address again, 21 Mill Pond Lane? I think that says read Mill Pond Street, we must be in the wrong place." Jim craned his neck, and even though the inside of the car was too dark to see discernable features, Charles knew his mouth was pointing down in that creaky old way—some parts of Jim always looked like they would be better on a man of advanced age. That was something nice about blonds, they could go white or gray without anyone ever really noticing, because what was the difference? There had been a little Cruella DeVille in him from the start. When Franny wasn't around, that was what Charles liked most about Jim, the frosty undercurrent of detachment.

The car was rolling along slowly, half a mile an hour. The

driveway was gravel, and the Saab snored loudly. The nearby houses were all lit up, nice big normal houses with roofs and proper kitchens and bathrooms and probably jet-skis in the garages. Franny opened the backdoor to the car and jumped out before either of the men could tell her not to, and went skipping up to the front door. She cupped her hands around her eyes and tried to look in through the door.

"No, this is it, this is it!" She spun around on her heels, the headlights of the car tracking her like a spotlight. She did a little pirouette on the porch, her dark pigtails twirling out to the side, and Jim stopped the car.

In the light, the house wasn't that bad—it was worse. There were three "bedrooms" lined up end to end, with one door leading straight to the next, like what newspaper ads politely called railroad apartments, but were in reality nothing more than glorified hallways. This house was no different. The three bedrooms were carved out of a single hall, leading down towards the dock. The fatter part of the house, the hand to the bedrooms' thumb, had been a quaint little cottage, once upon a time. The house did have three bedrooms. The house did have a dock. The house did have Massachusetts-appropriate knick-knacks on every available surface. What it didn't have: charm, clean towels, two forks that matched, pots with lids, anything remotely childproof, a full-length mirror, or level floorboards.

Franny and Charles drove Jim's car into town and bought some cheapo plastic lawn chairs. There were always more stores in the Vineyard than you ever remembered, more tiny little

Mom-and-Pop places that had grown from the ashes of other Mom-and-Pop places after the old people died and their kids decided to move to Boston to live like normal people, where peanut butter and toilet paper weren't overpriced imports. Bobby and Charles sat in the back, both strapped in like good little boys while Franny drove slowly through the streets.

"I swear, I thought he was going to kill you." Charles looked over at Bobby. How soon did children learn the word 'kill'? He smiled and kicked his feet around. He'd been running for what seemed like forever but didn't talk much. Everyone struggled to get a word in edgewise with Fran.

"Who?" Her sunglasses took up half her face, like something out of *Charlie's Angels*. Charlie's post-pregnancy-weight angel. Charlie's frozen custard angel. Charlie's fag-hag angel. Franny was mugging for him in the rear-view mirror. "Jim?"

"Is that his name?" She was bad, bad, bad. "I forget, I was too drunk at your wedding, I wasn't paying attention. Yes, Jimmmmm. You could have called the Better Business Bureau or the Vineyard Mounties or something, I'm sure there are other rentals, it's not a holiday weekend."

"And what fun would that have been?" She spied a parking spot, and yelped with joy. "See? We're having fun already!"

Bobby joined his mother in a laugh at his father's expense.

The shopping list wasn't very long, just some hamburger meat to go along with the fixings they'd packed in the trunk. They hadn't lied about the barbeque, although it looked as though it hadn't been cleaned since its date of inception. Franny thought it would lend some flavor, like a cast iron skillet. Jim pushed her aside and started the fire. Wine. A rubber ball and a flimsy kite for Bobby. More wine. Franny loved to shop, it hardly mattered where. She loved those stupid tourist shops with printed T-shirts and ashtrays, the stuff no one ever wants. She cooed over all of it—*Look, Charlie! It's a tiny little sandbox, only it's an ashtray and you put your cigarettes out in the sand!* Bobby exercised remarkable restraint. Charles encouraged her. They came home with a T-shirt for each of them, their two already on their backs and Jim's in Franny's lap, at the ready. Jim rolled his eyes and asked where the meat was. His wife handed over the drooping plastic bag and he took it inside to pummel and season, leaving Fran and Charles to open the wine.

The dock was twenty feet or so long, and Charles thought he'd set up his supplies there, maybe paint some picturesque water scenes with naked Bobby at the edge, Buddha belly extended. Franny always wanted to be painted as a bohemian, even though she'd left the sixties with her bra intact and hairless legs. Little Franny Gold. She always said she would have kept her name, or at least hyphenated it, if Gold-Post had sounded less like a slurring football announcer. The Golds lived on Eastern Parkway in what would have been a million-dollar apartment if it had been on Park Avenue, every surface dust-free, even if you showed up unannounced. The Golds would not have tolerated a bohemian.

"Don't draw pictures of me drinking, you're going to make me look like a wino." Franny's whole mouth was already purple. The wine was cheap and made their lips pucker, but only at first.

"Of course not," Charles said, finishing the bowl of the wine glass with a fat charcoal line.

Behind them, Jim stood with his back to the water, prodding the meat on the grill. A cool breeze rustled Charles' papers and sent tiny red sparks out from under the barbeque.

"Careful, Jim, we don't want to set the house on fire," Charles called out.

"You mean this is a 'before'? How could they tell the difference?" He was still mad. Once he ate, he would be better. He was like a teenager, sullen until his belly was full. Jim kept talking with his back to them, the conversation aimed at no one, all mumbled curse words.

"So, Charlie, I was thinking." She stage-whispered, cupping her hand around her mouth to block the sound from Jim, who wasn't listening anyway. "What do you think about smoking a little p-o-t?" She opened her eyes wide in mock surprise. "I know you brought some. He doesn't have to know."

"What about Bobby?" He was already asleep inside, taking the second of his two daily naps, a habit Charles fully intended to steal.

"Let's not tell him, more for us." She scrunched up her nose, sending little wavy lines of wickedness across her cheeks.

"You are so bad, Fran."

She nodded, and took another sip. Someone in a canoe slid by, gliding across the surface, and waved. Franny waved back, smiling. "Do be do be do." The dying sunlight was in her eyes, painting her skin a warmer color than it usually was. This is how Charles would paint her: this warm, this pink.

"Love you, Charlie," she said. She knew the light suited her. Whenever she felt particularly presentable or pleased with herself, Franny slipped into this Katherine Hepburn voice, all sass and class. For a slightly round Jewish girl from Brooklyn, that was pretty much the top of the heap.

Before the wedding, when Franny was cloistered away in some hidden chamber of the synagogue with her mother fixing every defiant hair on her head, Jim and Charles had sat alone in his dressing room, which also seemed to be the Hebrew school classroom. Charles leaned against the lip of the teacher's desk, and Jim sat opposite him in an orange plastic chair, the seat of which looked like it was made to hold a ten-year-old's slim hips and little else. Their suit jackets hung beside each other, the hangers hooked over the doorframe, two swaying old friends. Some people looked great in black suits, spruced-up and handsome, and Jim was one of them. Charles looked more like a waiter than Cary Grant, or even Warren Beatty.

It was three days after Passover, and the largest wall in the room was covered with hand-drawn interpretations of the Seder plate—one poor girl had been assigned the brown nutty stuff, and the drawing could easily have passed for what accumulates at the bottom of a rabbit's cage.

"Why is this night different from all other nights?" Jim squinted a little.

"Well, let's see, we're in a synagogue, you're marrying Franny…I'd say there are a shitload of reasons, wouldn't you?"

Jim smiled and pointed to the blackboard behind Charles, where his question was written in chalk.

"Oh, right. What can I say, the only holidays I ever celebrated had to do with birthdays, mine or Jesus." Charles said, seeming slightly embarrassed.

Outside, the sun was just starting to lower itself gently into the horizon. It wouldn't be much longer before Franny's father came to get them. All the Posts and the Golds and their friends were already assembled in the large room next door, waiting to bear witness to the blessed event. Charles tried to fix his hair in the small, waist-high mirror on the back of the door. The glass was covered with smudgy fingerprints, evidence that people had been there before, beaten him to the punch. Charles wondered how Fran was doing, if her mother was driving her crazy. He could imagine little Mrs. Gold wielding two aerosol cans, trying to shellac Franny's curls into quiet submission.

"Thanks for doing this, Charlie." Jim stood next to Charles' reflection in the mirror, their tuxedoed lower halves both cut off at the belly-button. "It means a lot. Having you here."

"Where else would I be?" The thought of Franny getting married without Charles seemed so wrong. They could have done it without Jim, maybe, but not without him. Who would she have talked to? They could have filled him in later, told him all his lines, how handsome he was. They would have looked into each other's eyes and known, yes, this was forever.

"I mean, I figure if you're standing up there, Fran probably won't run out the door." Jim shoved his hands in his pockets where they could twitch in peace. He was nervous.

"I don't think she'd run anyway." Charles turned to face him. Jim's eyes were boring a hole in the wooden floor, his eyebrows high wires across his forehead.

"No?"

"No way—too much energy. That's practically cardiovascular exercise. I think she'd just sneak out the back, you know, catch a cab."

Jim put his hand over his heart, wounded. "Guess I'm lucky you'll be there to stop her, then, huh?" He loved Franny, Charles could see that. Jim had the sense to love her, and so Charles had no choice but to love him, too. "I'd bring her right back."

Someone rapped their knuckles against the door. Franny was ready, and who were they to keep her waiting?

Bobby had to keep his shoes on whenever he was out of bed due to rusty nails and other miscellaneous dangers, which meant that each thundering little step was amplified. Fran and Jim took the proper bedroom, which left Charles to the bunk beds, which in turn left him with no sleep whatsoever. Dear thing that he was, Bobby was up at six every morning, running back and forth, hitting every loud spot in the floor. The walls, perhaps unsurprisingly, were made of a material that could best be described as loose-leaf paper, and so Charles at least knew for certain that he wasn't the only miserable grump in the house.

Franny woke when Bobby woke. She fed him some yogurt and bananas, which Charles knew because she sang him a little song while she was doing it, dictating every one of her movements. "And now I mash the bananas with my little fork, and here comes the yogie, a mush a mush a mush..." Franny could not then, nor could she ever, carry a tune, even one of her own invention. Charles could hear groaning from the other bedroom. Bobby finished breakfast, and before Charles knew what was happening, there was a song about cleaning off his face, there was a knock at the door, and then, like it or not, he was babysitting.

Charles was still half naked, half asleep, and almost entirely pissed off at Fran. But there Bobby was, little boy wonder, saying "Drawing?" and what could he do, really? He reached up his arms, asking plaintively for Charles to lift him up onto the creaky bottom bunk. His hair was still fair then, closer to Jim's color, and as he sat in front of Charles, waiting patiently for the art supplies to appear. Charles was struck by the fact that he and Bobby had remarkably similar hairlines. Wisps in the front, more solid cover in the back, long dangly bits on top that hung down across their foreheads; they were two marooned teenaged surfers who the undertow had cruelly spit up on the coast of balding.

The door to Fran and Jim's room slammed shut, which was a feat in and of itself, given that the door didn't weigh anything. Feet—Franny's—padded loudly across the floor, presumably towards the bed her husband was still sleeping in.

Most children are accustomed to hearing the sound of their parents' voices, in all sorts of situations. How else do children learn the meaning of words like 'yell' or 'scream' or 'bloody murder'? Bobby, clearly, was going to have no problem remembering any of the above. She'd always been a good fighter, but in the years she'd been married to Jim, Fran and Charles hadn't had any major arguments. Now he understood why; she was using that energy elsewhere.

In the next room, an object fell to the floor. It was a small object, nothing breakable, but nevertheless, it unleashed something powerful out of the slumbering Jim.

The last time Charles had heard them fight was when the three of them were all traveling to London together, three broke kids, and his tiny little shoebox of a room was right next to theirs, with a similarly thin wall. Jim and Charles were showering simultaneously, each in their own rooms, and when Charles flushed the toilet after his shower, Jim's water went ice cold, which Charles could tell from the angry yelp ringing through the wall. Across the room, Franny poured herself a glass of water from the tap, and she got blamed for what was clearly Charles' error in judgment. Jim screamed at her, sure that she had done it on purpose. They weren't so serious yet, and Franny loved to play games. She might have done it on purpose, and in any case, couldn't be sure that she hadn't ruined his shower accidentally. The only thing worse than hearing them argue was hearing them have sex, which usually followed. Of course, that was before Bobby.

They were trying not to yell at first, as it was quite clear that Charles could hear every word they were saying. Franny was more effective than her husband in this regard, probably because she cared that Charles knew that she was being yelled at, while Jim had no such reservation. One nice thing about being friends with a couple is that one usually gets to hear both sides of an argument, without hearing the argument itself, and so over the course of, say, ten years, you know them better than they know themselves, and with none of the pyrotechnics.

Sometimes, however, one finds one's self in the next bedroom, with nowhere to go, and nothing to do but listen.

Jim: *...this fucking bed...*
Franny:*...Bobby...*
Jim:*...and the fucking smile...*
Franny:*...adventure, my...*
Jim:*...about what I wanted...*
Franny:*...coo...*
Jim:*...no...*
Franny:*...yes!...*

This went on for several more minutes, increasing in volume with each point. When they were still courting, Jim and Franny used to fight everywhere: pizza parlors, bowling lanes, the office bathroom. It was something they liked about each other. Charles wanted the opposite: *find someone calm*, that's what he said to himself. Ferdinand the Bull was the ideal mate—tough on the outside, soft on the inside, and the opposite of both Jim and Fran. It just wasn't worth it.

Jim:*...and then you and Charlie...*
Franny:*...oh, Jim, please...*
Jim:*...and the fucking house...*
Franny:*...but love...*
Jim:*...fucking drunks, at least...*
Franny:*...don't you dare...*
Jim:*...at least Charlie's...*

Here's where Jim called Charles a faggot. He'd done it before, Charles knew, and liked to think that they could say things like that to one another, after all, Charles had slept in the same bed as his wife nearly as many times as he had before they got married. They were family, Jim must have thought, it was okay. It was entirely different, however, to hear it through the wall, when none of Jim's wry charm was attached, and when, technically, Charles wasn't listening. Franny, to her credit, went ballistic, literally bouncing off pieces of furniture like a ricocheted bullet, her voice higher and tinnier than usual. She sounded like a Chihuahua trapped in an overheated car, bless her. There were other words that bothered her more, *moist,* inexplicably, and *kike,* which no one even used anymore, but *faggot* was pretty high on her list.

Meanwhile, Bobby had put down the Cray-Pas and pushed aside the sheet of newsprint he and Charles been sharing, crumpling its corners with his sneakered feet as he lay down with his head in Charles' lap, bringing his tiny little fist up to the ear not already muffled by Charles' shin.

After a few minutes, the paper-y door opened and slammed again, softer footsteps this time. Jim padded down the hall, still in his cotton pajamas—so old-fashioned, like somebody's father, which of course he already was, although it was funny to think about Bobby growing up to be an actual person and not just a downy little lump made in Franny's image. The Saab rumbled awake, and he drove off, erasing the driveway in one easy stroke. Where could he go in his pajamas, really? He couldn't get out of the car. He probably didn't have his wallet. Charles was just starting to imagine Jim getting pulled over, going ninety on some tiny little beach road, and having to explain to the officer that his license and registration were in his pants, in his room, in his crappy rental house. The cop would understand, of course. Jim was a man's man, all about the unspoken codes of macho-ness. The cop had a wife, too. He would recognize the color in Jim's cheek, the sleep still in his eyes, and he would send him off without even a warning, maybe even tell him about a particularly good route for some angry driving.

There was a knock on the door. Franny was too upset to be shy about crying. Her whole face was red and damp, like some kind of Goya midwife, dark and angry.

"Want to go for a swim, duckies?" She laughed, and it was a little bit snotty; she had to blow her nose. Bobby pushed himself up onto all fours and wagged his bottom like a tail. Franny walked over to the bed and scooped him up in her arms. Her forearm brushed against Charles' leg, and she looked at him, smiling. "It's okay," she said, to both of them, and to herself. "Mommy's okay, mommy's okay."

The water below the dock was warm enough for swimming, at least in the sunshine. Bobby treated the entire crumbling thing like a pirate ship, full of hidden treasures and things that were good by virtue of their very dangerous nature. He was so straight, even then. Franny and Charles had talked about Bobby growing up to be gay, what the likelihood was. He just wasn't, though. It was easy enough to tell. He liked balls and bats and running and farts and his father's car.

The sand was more like dirt, rocky like the rest of New England and nothing special. Franny and Charles kept their shoes on to wade in, two pairs of canvas sneakers ballooning in size under the water. They were looking for wildlife, but they seemed to be the only specimens out so early.

"He's funny, you know," Fran said, facing Bobby, who was jumping off the dock into his mother's arms, again and again. He bent his knees and jumped straight up, his tiny back pushing itself forward as though his spine could come right through his ribs. He shot himself like a cannon was behind him, every appendage flying.

"What, you mean all that fag stuff? That really is funny. He should quit the *Review* and do stand-up, don't you think?" The water was waist high, and the upper half of Charles' body was trying its best to cultivate the kind of tan that would make the trip worthwhile.

"Come on, I'm being serious." Franny made an 'oof' sound as she caught Bobby in her arms, sending him into a peal of laughter. "I'm sorry you had to hear us. We really don't do it that often, that kind of yelling, I mean." She was lying, which was alright. It was her marriage, after all. "It's just that, you know..." Bobby ran back down the pier to fetch a plastic truck the size of his head. "Everything is different now."

"You're not, though. And neither is he, really." Charles' voice was angrier than he wanted it to be. "You're still hilarious and he's still a Yalie WASP with a stick up his ass. And I mean that in the least fun way possible."

"Not in front of Bobby." Franny opened her arms for the flying little body. Bobby's feet hit the water, a surprise bonus.

Splash splash splash. Franny twirled his tight frame around in a circle, dragging his feet across the surface of the water, sending ripples outwards into the big, wide world, of which Bobby was the center. She had someone else to take care of now.

The Saab and its master purred back up the driveway around eleven. Jim had, apparently, had the time to put on a pair of jeans and a T-shirt before peeling off, and so he could have gotten out of the car to stretch his legs, buy a newspaper, eat breakfast. Charles should have known. Jim was never one to leave things to chance, he was too well turned out for things like that. He always put his wallet in the same place, his passport, his keys, his whatever. Even their medicine cabinet was organized. It was easy to tell which things were his: the muscle-balm, the vitamins. As far as Charles knew, Jim had never had indigestion, diarrhea, constipation, insomnia, depression, hives, warts, or pimples. Walking back in from the car, with the sun shining right on the top of his head like a goddamn golden halo, even Charles could tell why Franny loved him. He was like a living, breathing cologne advertisement. He should have ridden horses and played polo.

Bobby took one look at his father and was off and running, one two three, straight into Jim's arms. Charles thought it might possible that things would have wound up differently; with Jim softening into imperfection, but watching him with Bobby, whom he tossed into the air with all the passion of a ten-buck-an-hour babysitter, he doubted it.

Franny waded back in, leaving Charles alone in the water. It was warmer now, with the sun more directly overhead. He drifted backwards to float on his back, his canvas toes splaying out to the sides like wayward rudders. Charles watched as Franny tugged her swimsuit out of her bottom, adjusting herself for whatever Jim was about to say. She hadn't washed her hair, or even brushed it, and even the wet parts were flattened at weird angles. The water moved Charles slowly back, back, into the ocean. He wondered how long he could float before hitting something: a passing boat, Africa. His ears slipped above and below the surface, filling up with glugs and noises from the watery depths. Charles could have heard what they were saying to each other, but he didn't. She'd tell him later, putting the emphasis on whatever she felt had been the most submissive, gentle thing Jim had said. In her version, she wouldn't have had that look on her face, or the pouty lip, that much Charles knew for sure. Sometimes it was best to let people believe what they want to about themselves, especially Franny, who was held together with barbed wire and a thick coating of cream-cheese frosting. One of the houses nearby had a flag up, nothing he recognized, some secret sailing message going out to the initiated, and it waved lazily in the wind. You and me, it was saying, you and me. Fuck them. Stay in the water.

Back at the office, they'd all had a great time. Franny'd had the best time of all, of course. You could hear her laugh from anywhere in the office, even from Charles' desk, which was on the floor below. She would pull someone aside, anyone, it hardly mattered, and start to tell them a story in a whisper, but by the time she got to the end she'd be speaking at full-volume, hoping to cull more listeners. Everyone liked to be singled-out, and so by the end of the following week, Franny had special little tête-à-têtes with half the staff, including the cleaning ladies. Charles would walk by her in the hall on his way to the big color Xerox and she and her big, red mouth would be performing something out of *Gypsy*, all for the benefit of Nena from Ecuador.

Usually, for lunch, they walked over to one of the delis with the enormous sandwiches. Sure, there were always tourists and flashbulbs, but the potato pancakes covered in sour cream and applesauce would make you forget. As her best friend, maybe Charles should have tried to help Franny watch her waistline, but he was still mad, having spent the five-hour drive back to the city listening to her laugh uproariously at Jim's every syllable. He didn't care if she ended up wearing bed sheets.

Charles ordered a cream soda and pastrami. Franny got the tuna, which he supposed was the diet choice on the menu, but they gave you so much of it that it was roughly equivalent to eating an entire jar of mayonnaise. The ancient waitresses stuck straws and pens in their aprons and made smacking sounds with their gigantic lip-sticked mouths, pausing only to silently scold people when they ordered white bread instead of rye. Even when everything was in tip-top shape, though, and the rabble was behaving itself, they never moved very quickly. Perhaps they put that in the ad, *must have wide hips and move like an elephant.*

"I really am sorry about Jim." Franny's mouth stretched open to jam in a corner of her sandwich. The flimsy pieces of bread of the top and bottom of the tunafish bowling ball didn't stand a chance, nor did Franny's skirt, which acted as an impromptu safety net for falling pieces of wet, salty fish.

"As in, sorry you married a bigot?" He plunked a fallen piece of pastrami into his mouth and washed it down. "Or, like, sorry I had to hear it?"

She gave him a look. A round tourist and his equally round wife jostled past their table, no, towards their table, and sat down at the adjacent two seats, which put them about three centimeters away from Franny and Charles' elbows.

"No, like sorry he was such an asshole. I really mean it." Fran had stopped eating, and had her hands clasped in front of her chest. "When he married me, he married you, you know what I mean? He shouldn't have said it, simple as that."

Their neighbors to the left were from Germany. The husband had a Minolta around his neck on a bright yellow strap, all the easier for the thieves to spot. His wife held the map. Charles wondered if she thought she would still need it, to find the bathroom or maybe her way out. He almost couldn't believe they were there—the second-most famous Jewish deli in the city. Some kind of reparations, he supposed. *Oh, fraulein, let's order the pastrami and set things right.* They were dressed somewhere in archetypal tourist fashion—shorts and hiking boots, but with knotted sweaters tied around their shoulders, should a chill appear later in the day. No doubt they had umbrellas in their rucksacks. Charles imagined he and Franny dressed up like that, with baseball hats and thick socks, tromping around some foreign place, their sunglasses too large for their faces. She would hold the map, and he would paint her portrait in a thousand tiny towns. Charles looked across the table and smiled. Fran returned the smile, her mouth open and wide, with beige flecks of tuna wedged in between almost every tooth. She was a total wreck, and he loved every inch of her. He wasn't her husband, or her son, or her officemate. Charles got the sunny side of her, the good face; the best bits were always for him.

PUTTANESCA

Laura and Stephen were set up by their therapist. It was after they'd both quit going to their bereavement support groups, and didn't seem any weirder than being set up by your divorce lawyer, which had happened to a couple of Laura's girlfriends. Rose suggested they meet at a Starbucks, somewhere public, where hostility and anger weren't allowed. Laura picked the one closest to her job at the magazine; she often saw blind dates take place there, nervous conversations with too much talk about the exes. It was the working girl's way of multi-tasking: screening potential suitors on their lunch breaks. She picked an empty table with a view of the street, and kept her sunglasses on so that she could scrutinize all the single men with impunity. Three were bald, which would have been fine. One had glasses and a weedy frame; surely that was him; she'd described John to Rose. Would she send her a replacement husband, as though John had been an ill-fitting sweater, finally swapped for the correct size?

One guy looked like a quarterback and began wandering around in between the tables after buying his venti latte. She watched him circle the other tables of single women, who stayed focused on their laptops. He was tall, over six feet, and looked like the kind of boy who'd had lots of girlfriends in high school. He had probably been on the lacrosse team, or soccer, something sun-kissed and surrounded by cheering fans. It had never rained where he grew up, she just knew it. Laura slid her sunglasses to the top of her head.

"Stephen?" she said, sure that she would be speaking into thin air, that the quarterback would shake his head and probably laugh when he got outside. Laura wasn't unattractive, she knew, but hers was a subtler kind: unplucked eyebrows and sensible footwear.

He looked startled, like a baby next to a popped balloon just before the tears started to flow. But then the momentary look of panic was gone, so absent, in fact, that Laura was sure she'd imagined it. "Laura?" he said. Stephen was already smiling when he slid into the seat across from her, as easily as if she and everyone else at the Starbucks had somehow wandered into his living room.

"Looks that way," Laura said. Her hair felt even more brown than usual, like mouse-fur or dry dirt. "Hi." At least it was long again. After John died, she'd chopped all her hair off, up to her ears. Her mother said she looked like Joan of Arc, who Laura thought probably didn't have a mirror. It had not been a compliment.

"Nice to meet you," Stephen said. His teeth were beautiful products of adolescent orthodontia: straight and well spaced. Rose hadn't mentioned the teeth. In fact, Rose hadn't mentioned anything, other than that Stephen too had lost his wife, and was chafing at the uniformity of the (aged, female) participants of the bereavement group he'd been attending. She definitely hadn't mentioned his shoulders, or his lion's mane, which crested and cooed at Laura as though it had a voice all its own, each blond curl telling her why this couldn't, wouldn't, shouldn't work.

Laura had been to Rome before, some ten years previous, with John. They hadn't yet married, but the trip, in the honeymoon of their relationship, was overflowing with the kind of romance that nauseates fellow travelers with all its public kisses and fondling. But that was a long time ago, and Laura felt almost certain she was ready to go back. After all, Rome been around for centuries and centuries without her, and without John, and surely it wouldn't bear the mark of his loss. She would have to do that alone, and hope that Rome didn't recognize the scar and offer her damp, sorry weather in return. If she wasn't ready now, then she might never be, and better to try than to stay home with the cat.

After pushing for a Roman holiday for several months, Stephen was excited, and booked a room in a boutique hotel on the Piazza in front of the Pantheon. It was a small building, only five stories high, with only two hotel rooms per floor. They were on the very top. Outside their window, the dome of the Pantheon arched gracefully into the sky, until the roof itself opened up, as though the two couldn't stand to be apart a moment longer. The hotel was expensive, more than five hundred dollars a night, but Stephen paid happily. He'd been rich his whole life, and found the idea of money rather embarrassing. In truth, the room probably cost even more than he had admitted.

The hotel clerk had one good eye, one bad. The one on the left looked at them, and the one on the right examined the crown molding. He explained to them the concept of the elevator. They tried to catch the good eye and nod, letting him know they understood.

"The door—the door, yes?" He pointed, jabbing a short finger in the direction of the elevator shaft. Laura and Stephen nodded in unison. "The door close, or elevator no move. Door close. Must close!" He wagged the finger again, for emphasis. "Must close!" The good eye narrowed; he doubted them already. His finger looked like an Italian sausage, full of red bloody specks. He must have been in his mid-seventies; Laura wondered what he was doing there. Even if he owned the hotel, surely there was a son, a grandson, someone who could do this for him. The good eye found her staring, and forced her into retreat. Laura shuffled with her bags into the small cabin of the elevator, repeating what he had said. "We'll close the door, we'll close it, I promise," she said. Stephen ducked in just before the door began to shut.

After showering off the remains of the recycled air of the airplane, they decided a walk was in order. It was a Saturday, and sunny if not warm, a perfect day to explore a new city. Stephen, for all of his traveling, had never made it to Rome, an oversight he'd spent the last three months planning to correct. He was armed with books and lists and maps and tickets to the Borghese. His digital camera was brand-new and could hold five hundred photos.

"Do you want some coffee? Some cappuccino? I hear it's good here," he said. Stephen put his hand around her waist and tugged her closer to him. Laura's hair pulled slightly under his grip. "Whaddya say? You hungry?"

Laura shrugged. There was a cool breeze coming through the street, bouncing off the stone walls. She didn't remember there being so much stone. "I could have some cappuccino. Why not, right? It's still morning, isn't it?"

"If not here, then somewhere." He kissed the top of her head, sending her chin into his shoulder with a clunk. Stephen looked ahead, beaming, while Laura detangled herself and gave her face a rub.

It was in fact already noon, and by the time they'd been walking for half an hour, the smell of lunch was too seductive to ignore, pouring heavily out of doors and windows. According to the guidebooks, lunch could be a three-course meal, even for real Italians. Laura's stomach began to growl; she could hear it over the din of the mopeds and the buses and the tourists.

"Let me see the book, what are we close to?" she said.

Stephen dutifully dug one of the guidebooks out of his coat pocket and handed it over.

"Do those look like tortoises? On that fountain? I think we're here," she said, pointing to a spot on the map. "What does that mean in terms of my stomach?" Laura flipped the page. Stephen leaned in and looked over her shoulder. On the fountain behind them, enormous stone turtles—tortoises, although she wouldn't have known the difference if the book hadn't told her—were climbing out of the water basin.

"Ah, I know where we are. Here, right, let's go, fried artichokes." Some part of her had known where she was going, the heel of her left foot, maybe, or the tip of her nose. Something remembered.

Stephen spun around on his heels, looking up for street signs. "Right," he said, "this way."

"I know it's that way, I just said so." Laura shut the book and tucked it in her bag, walking ahead down the narrow sidewalk.

The Jewish Ghetto was something Laura hadn't expected to find twice in Rome, not by accident. After all, Rome was Catholic, what with the Pope a stone's throw, and all those churches, churches, churches. But she and John had found it, just like this, tripping along the tiny little streets with unwieldy maps protruding from their bags and blisters growing happily on their toes. It had been summertime, the middle of August, when rates were cheaper and everything seemed so ripe it was bound to spoil. They had been on this street, D'Ottavia, she remembered it now. Looking back, all these little streets had run together, all the piazzas had become one enormous open space, all with olive-skinned teenagers necking like crazy, and them, too—they hadn't been so much older. They had held hands on every one of these streets, kissed fingers and necks and cheeks across tables at the nicest restaurants they could afford, which weren't really very nice at all, but they didn't care. John had always loved to kiss her in public, something that Laura couldn't imagine anymore, feeling so strongly about the inside of someone else's mouth that she wouldn't mind irritating the people around her.

A waiter wearing a white coat showed them to a table. She didn't remember the restaurant being so fancy. Laura and Stephen both took the folded napkins off their empty plates and put them on their laps, hidden from each other but not from the passers-by. John had always liked sitting in the window, too, like some kind of puppet-show. *Look at me accumulate crumbs in my napkin, look at me drop my knife, look at me hold his hand.* She and Stephen wouldn't be holding hands under the table, though. They were past that. It had been nearly a year and a half. It still felt wrong to say boyfriend, which made her feel like a lusty teenager. Thirty-five was too old to have a boyfriend. Some of her unmarried friends had taken to borrowing the homosexual-sounding parlance 'partner,' which always made Laura roll her eyes and give a little cough. Sometimes the word 'ex-husband' came out of her mouth, and people would roll their eyes, ready to commiserate, they had one too, and she would have to say, no, no, he died, he's dead. Stephen would lower his eyes and pet her arm, always supportive, but she just wanted to say, 'Don't you get that I would still be married?' So mostly she just called him her husband, and if people thought she meant Stephen, well, that was fine. His face always colored slightly with the notion.

They ordered the artichokes and the house pasta, *cacio e pepe*, cheese and pepper. Stephen ordered a bottle of white off of the wine list, and then some veal Milanese, a nice oily start to the afternoon. Stephen preferred French food, and they were always eating something or other provençal. When the artichokes arrived, the neighborhood specialty, a pang of something stronger than hunger hit Laura square in the gut. It was too much, sitting in this room, tasting the same taste, looking out at the same street. She was two-timing herself, covering her discarded artichoke leaves with fresher ones, still crisp from the frying oil—John wouldn't say that he minded, couldn't, but she knew, and that was bad enough. If he'd been there, sitting across the street, watching them, he would have picked up a rock and thrown it through the window. He would still be young and impetuous. Laura was glad she didn't know the Italian word for prostitute. It was probably beautiful, too beautiful for the way she felt. She wondered if Italian whores ate artichokes, or if they had a dish all their own.

"Delicious, huh?" Stephen shoveled a forkful of something creamy into his mouth. He was more handsome than John. She could say that. Next to Stephen, Laura was always aware of where the real beauty was in her relationship. Her friends, sweetly, had tried in vain to stifle their surprise when she'd introduced him.

He was right; it was delicious. Everything Laura put in her mouth tasted like it ought to have been there before. Maybe food was the same as people, and got more attractive the more you were exposed.

"Is this bacon?" Stephen held up a fork—something brown and glistening teetered on the tines.

"I guess so. Does it taste like bacon?"

He popped it in his mouth and chewed. "Tastes like a gift from God."

"So what's the problem?"

Stephen looked around. Two other parties sat in the dining

room, but no one was at a directly adjacent table. Everyone else was speaking Italian and laughing. "Isn't this basically a no-no? Bacon? I mean, this place is Jewish, right?"

It was an honest question. "How am I supposed to know? I think being Italian trumps not eating pork products, maybe. I'll be right back." Laura dropped her napkin onto her plate and walked around the restaurant until she found the bathroom, where she sat down on the toilet and cried.

It had taken months for the details to emerge: Stephen hadn't actually been married. They—he and Jane, the marathon runner, the blonde, the mourned—hadn't even been engaged. He told Laura carefully. It had been easier, he explained, to say that they were married. The old ladies in the bereavement group had taken him to task. Not only was he young, only in his late thirties, but he also hadn't married the girl. What were they supposed to support, his indifference? His unwillingness to commit? Laura didn't want to admit feeling some of the same resentment, but she knew what it meant. Despite his sadness, which she did not dismiss, Laura knew that Stephen wanted what he'd never had: a wife.

Tuesday was even cooler weather than they'd expected, only fifty degrees. They walked down the Via del Condotti and watched Japanese tourists lumber under the weight of their shopping bags. The window displays weren't as elaborate as they were in New York, but Laura didn't object—it seemed like the Romans didn't have to do as much convincing. In one window, a leather suitcase the size of an entire cow sat by itself, patiently waiting for someone to buy so much extra clothing that they needed it to carry their belongings home.

In front of them, two women in skintight jeans and high heels stabbed the sidewalk with an aggressive pace. Laura had always thought of herself as a fast walker, but these women, in four-inch heels, put her to shame. Of course, she didn't know where she was going.

"Want to duck in here, maybe?" Stephen gestured toward an open doorway. The store seemed to be made entirely out of glass and white plastic, like something from the future. Laura wondered if they'd had to tear down whatever gorgeous, ancient building had been there to put this in, but then she noticed that the walls and ceiling were actually still intact, the moldings and the carved putti hovering over the doorway outside, the angels of commerce. It only looked like something new, but really it was the same as all the others.

"Sure, why not? When in Rome, right?" Laura liked this joke when she was at home, and being pressured into doing something, but when the pun came out of her mouth, she felt nauseated, and like she was trying entirely too hard for something she didn't want in the first place.

"Exactly." Stephen took her by the elbow and led her into the shop.

An Italian woman roughly Laura's age approached them, her hands clasped in front of her chest like a nun. Her dark brown hair was wound into an elaborate chignon, so expert it looked professionally done. Shopgirls must make more money here, Laura thought. Commission. No wonder she looks like she's praying.

But before Laura could even finish thinking about all the money she wouldn't spend, Stephen recited some Italian phrase. Laura's neck swiveled quickly, trying to see the words as they left his mouth. Had he been practicing in the bathroom? They had been together for the last three days non-stop. She tried to catalogue all the times he'd been away from her: showers, bathroom time at home and at restaurants, that was it. She could see it, though, the moment she got up in the middle of the night to pee, he'd whip out his phrasebook from under the bed and try furiously to memorize something without saying it aloud.

The salesgirl nodded, and beckoned for them to follow. The store was full of clothing, leather goods, shoes. What had he asked for? Laura had heard of the designer, everyone had—come to think of it, Laura had first read about them on the pages of the magazine in a piece she'd edited, something about 'the new luxury.' In a brief, horrifying flash, a four-digit number appeared in her mind's eye. She began to sweat a little.

The woman showed them to a wall of purses, although it seemed a shame to call them that, like something one's mother would bring on the cross-town bus. These were something else entirely, a class of handbag Laura had never encountered up close. Stephen pointed to one, an oversized shoulder bag with shiny buckles where the straps connected to the body. The woman took it off the shelf—it had lived in its own cubicle, practically the size of her apartment, Laura thought—and placed it on a glass case in front of them. Despite herself, Laura reached out to touch it. It was buttery soft, the color of creamy cappuccino. She ran her hand along the length of it, sliding her fingers over the polished buckles. She and John had spent days wandering the streets of Rome without ever going into a store like this. They'd sat on park benches and played in the grass like children. The larger part of Laura's brain knew what something like this would do to her, and to Stephen, what it would mean.

"You like it?" Stephen looked at her expectantly. He'd been practicing. He knew what to ask for, what this thing in front of her was called. He knew its name.

"It's astounding, actually, but I really can't let you buy this for me." The leather felt cherished, something you would keep forever, and then your children would fight over it. She wanted it. She would never use it, just keep it in its bag, surrounded by tissue paper, or no, she would use it every day, no one would ever see her without it. Even when she went running in Prospect Park, it would be like a third arm, only with pockets.

Stephen gently set his credit card down on the counter, and nodded. The salesgirl had seen this sort of interaction before, and didn't raise an eyebrow. Laura wondered what she was thinking, but didn't know how to stop what had already been put in motion, She imagined stamping her feet and walking out of the store, saying something like *how dare you*, making all of the other shoppers turn and stare. Instead she just watched with her mouth slightly open as the bag was wrapped and decorated like a Christmas tree, and tried to smile.

Laura liked to think that she knew a little about poetry, and it seemed appropriately redemptive to leave the crowded sidewalks and glossy storefronts for a dark apartment. The John Keats house was right next to the Spanish Steps, just a bit further down the street. They walked in the small side-door and up a flight of stairs, Laura still clutching her shopping bag as if to ward off thieving poets, dead or alive. She could always sell it later, she thought. It didn't really mean anything to her, not like the inexpensive wedding band she'd worn for years, a year even after John's death.

The museum was small, only a few rooms, and even those rooms were mostly just bookshelves. Laura and Stephen circled each other, moving in and out of each small room, stopping here and there to examine a poem mounted on the wall, or a lock of hair in a glass case. Keats had only lived there a few months, while trying to stave off the inevitable, and so there weren't very many of his things to gawk at—it wasn't like Graceland, where Laura had once looked at every object and thought, that was Elvis's toothbrush, that was Elvis's ashtray.

The smallest room, overlooking the steps, was where he had actually died. There was a plaque—*In this room/ on the 23rd of February 1821/ died/ John Keats*, so she knew for sure. Laura reached that room first, while Stephen was reading some Byron in the gift shop. In spite of the swanky location, and the view of the Bernini fountain below, Laura thought it did look like a room in which someone would die. It was narrow, with little more than a bed. His friends would have had to crouch beside him, or to pull in a chair from another room. There were letters he had written, his longhand still sharp and angled—did someone come in and help prop him up, tuck a firm pillow behind his back? He had been young, even younger than *her* John, who she had always imagined as the youngest person who ever died, as though the amount of unfairness would increase if there were no one younger. His loss had been the greatest squandering.

It took her a few minutes to notice the death mask. It was in a small glass cube, floating on a piece of dark, cherry wood, suitably somber. His eyes were closed, his lips slightly parted. His nose was large and curved. The pale color—even more white than ivory—looked about right. He probably hadn't eaten in days. He hadn't seen the sun in weeks; the curtains had kept his skin from the light, which would have hurt his eyes. Laura had seen it. She had sat right here, in this chair, beside this bed, held John's hand while it sweat and twitched. Cancer wasn't so different from consumption, really. You were still being eaten alive from the inside out. Laura shut her eyes when she heard footsteps. Stephen was a large man, and his footfalls were heavy, always announcing his arrival. John had been quiet, a shadow from the beginning.

"At least it was gradual," Stephen said. "He knew what was coming." He was talking about Keats, but Laura was still sitting by her John's bed, holding her husband's cold hand.

Jane, the blonde, the good, the dead, had gone quickly. This was a dangerous patch of ice they sometimes skated across, too thin to support their combined weight. "Better to be hit by a bus," she said. "Then all anyone can remember is how gorgeous you were, how effervescent and funny. This way, it's like dying all day long, every day, and everyone who loves you get to watch as bits and pieces chip off." She pointed to the death mask. "Do you think that's how he looked? His cheeks all sunken and jowly? He was a kid!" In the first months after John's death, before she started seeing Rose, Laura had gone to some meetings for widows held at the Y nearest her house. She was the youngest by nearly fifty years. She didn't know what they were complaining about, these old women, who'd had entire lives with their husbands, babies, babies who'd had babies. All she had were some poems he'd written in college, his books, his clothes, a few years, and his early death.

"I guess you're right," Stephen said, swallowing. He didn't always take the bait. In the dark room, his blond curls looked like hiding places for secret objects, tiny treasures. Laura thought he looked like Batman, his handsome face a series of planes all leading up to his strong chin. It was the sort of chin a boxer would love.

Laura and Stephen had been dating nearly six months before Laura wanted to have sex. John had been her first, her only, and just getting over the weirdness of it all took longer than she expected. Every time she and Stephen would be tangled up on the couch, making out fully clothed, she would feel his erection through his pants and she would have to leave. She just wasn't sure she could go through with it.

The day it happened, John had been dead for three years and seven months. Jane the blonde and good had been gone half as long. They only needed to do it once, and Laura remembered, *oh, right.* Then she wanted to have sex all the time. Not only was it fun, but it was an excellent way to get Stephen to stop looking at her with those green eyes, too green for her. All of a sudden, she didn't feel like just a widow anymore, the walking reminder to all of her friends and colleagues that they, too, would die someday, or, even worse, have to be saddled with this kind of loss. She bought a new lipstick, and lost five pounds. Everyone told her how good she looked, even John's mother, who must have guessed the reason.

Hotels were always the best. They made Laura feel like she could be anyone, he could be anyone, they could be in love. Other people had used those beds for the same reason, she knew. They'd been to a resort in the Catskills, a motel by the beach in Montauk, an inn in San Francisco. Rome was the furthest afield. Stephen knew better than to try it at her place.

The travel editor at the magazine had typed up a list of restaurants, romantic spots where one could eat al fresco and drink grappa beneath the swaying branches of a tree incongruously growing out of a patch of cobblestones. Stephen had stapled the list to the inside cover of one of their city guides, folding it up like a passed note in Geometry class. This one had been on the top of the list, both on the page and in the book itself. The reviews mentioned marriage proposals and homemade gnocchi. Laura was hoping for the latter. They were shown to a table in the corner of the patio, which was illuminated almost entirely by a trio of votive candles floating in a small dish of water.

"Seems a little church-y, doesn't it?" Stephen gestured towards the tiny flames between them. "Do you think people spontaneously burst into 'Ave Maria' during the cheese course?"

"I think it's all the cheese course, Stephen, we're in Italy."

He raised a finger. "You may be right."

The table was wide between them, an expanse of wood the size of a door, which it might have been in a previous incarnation. A waiter appeared beside them, followed swiftly by a bottle of red wine.

Stephen slid his knife and fork out of his way, and pushed the tip of his pointer finger into the neighborhood of the candles' light. His hair looked darker than usual, less boyish. He would be forty soon, and although they hadn't talked about it, Laura knew what came after thirty-nine.

"Listen, Laura," he started. "Look."

She looked. Stephen drew back his finger, as though he though wax might have jumped onto his skin from below, as though a burn might have appeared.

"Listen." Was she supposed to look, or listen? Laura thought about her eyes and ears taking smoke-breaks while the others worked. The ears would sun-tan, the eyes would nap. They'd all sit around the pool and flirt. Stephen began to stutter a bit. "I'm sorry about what happened today. At the house. I mean, I'm sorry about what I said. I know it's hard for you, when you're thinking about John, I mean. I don't want to disrespect that. I hope you know that. You know that, right?"

Stephen had said John's name a total of four times, ever. Each time it came out of his mouth, Laura felt like she'd been caught shoplifting. This was number five. Laura began to respond, but Stephen raised his hand a few inches off the table. He wasn't finished. Laura felt her chin turn slightly to one side, like a dog who has heard a high-pitched noise, and might have to run.

"I want you to know that, because it's true. But I also need you to understand that I only paid for two of us to come on this vacation."

Laura sucked her lips into her mouth.

"I don't want to upset you, really, I don't."

Laura nodded, sucked harder. A waiter appeared and Stephen shooed him away.

"It's just that we talked about this. This trip, I mean. And I thought everything was going to be okay, that you were fine."

"I am fine." Her eyes shone. She wanted it to be true, to prove him wrong.

Laura reached down beside her chair and put her shopping bag on her lap. The bag lived in a bag of its own, a soft cotton meant to protect it from the outside world, from anything that could hurt it. Laura's hands felt too large for her body, too masculine to own such an object. Surely she was doing something wrong. Stephen brought his fist to his mouth, as though he was about to chew on his knuckle.

There was enough crinkly tissue paper in the shopping bag to fill out the leather one, and Laura busily stuffed everything inside, and hooked the full bag over her shoulder. She smiled at Stephen, offering her teeth as a sign that all was well with the world. If something was wrong, he'd have to get past those teeth to find it.

It was three bottles later when they made it back to the hotel. The cock-eyed desk clerk rose from behind the concierge to let them in—the door was locked after midnight, and it was almost two. After shuffling noisily to the door, the clerk made a big show of removing a medieval-looking key from his belt. He lowered the key into place, releasing unseen levers and pulleys, and slowly swung the door open. Laura clutched her bag in front of her chest, beaming with her purple mouth. "Bwhoa-nah no-tay," she said, repeating something she had heard that sounded about right.

"Close door," he reminded them as they ducked into the elevator, already starting to paw at each other's clothes. "If no, I climb..." He mimed walking up the five flights of stairs to their room. "No good." His bad eye went towards the ceiling, as if already seeing what was to come.

When the elevator reached the fifth floor, Stephen led Laura into their room backwards, somehow unlocking the door without even looking behind him. Laura wondered if he'd been practicing that, too, the way kids practice kissing on their hands, on their pillows, eyes closed and concentrating. She stumbled over something and then realized it was her new bag, which she had unceremoniously dropped, forgetting what it was, and how much it cost. She screamed a little, but her mouth was directly on Stephen's, and the sound just went somewhere inside him, down into his lungs where it would turn around and come back as something else, something nicer, a happy moan.

They fell onto the bed: first Stephen, then Laura. His belt-buckle clanged onto the floor, his pants weighed down by pockets full of ticket stubs and receipts. Her skirt was a deflated inner-tube around her waist, trying to keep her afloat.

"Hey," Stephen said into her bare stomach. "I was thinking,"

"Bad idea. Really bad idea." Laura rolled him over and

straddled his torso with her legs. She let her hair swing down into his face, waves crashing against the rocky shore.

The phone rang, and Laura picked it up without even realizing it. It was almost five, she saw, and she was almost entirely still asleep.

"If you no close door, nothing move. Yes?"

Laura tried to understand. There were glimpses of something that made sense, pieces the dark room couldn't quite help her connect. She didn't close the door. She didn't close the door. Ah! It came to her all at once, the bad eye looking upwards, the backwards walk from the elevator. They hadn't shut the door to the cabin, and the elevator was stuck on their floor. No doubt someone was trying to rush to the airport, ringing insistently for the elevator, and finally, in a flush of anger, they'd called the front desk.

"I'm so sorry," she said, mumbling. "I'll close it right now. So sorry."

Laura let her feet hit the floor one by one, testing the water. The room was cold—they'd left the window open, and all of her clothing was still on the floor where it had dropped. Laura hunched her shoulders and balled her fists, hurrying to the hallway, her joints creaky and heavy with sleep. The one room opposite her own was quiet, with no light peeking out from under the door. They were asleep, her neighbors. She wondered if they were American too, if the desk clerk had scolded them as well, or if she were the only one who looked unhinged enough to do something so selfish, so wrong. She shut the elevator door and heard it immediately whir into motion, dropping down to rescue someone below. She stayed in the hallway for a moment, her body covered with goose bumps, and listened to the sounds of things progressing as they should. Someone needed to go home, someone needed a ride. She was in their way, and she hadn't even noticed.

Across the piazza, the Pantheon was gray and massive, a monument to hope. Laura looked back towards the bed, where Stephen had strewn himself across the bed like their clothes were thrown across the floor, at strange angles, as though he was taking up as much space as possible. The pale top sheet curled around his thighs, disappearing off behind him. Laura lifted the blanket off the floor, where it had landed, and curled her body against his, finding there to be enough space, after all. She covered them both with the thin down quilt and put her face back against the pillow.

Some six months before the trip, Laura and Stephen decided together that they would stop seeing Rose. Her interest in them had changed; they both felt it. And they were tired of starting most of their sentences, "Well, Rose said…" or "As I said to Rose…" Laura often thought that her own sessions with Rose were now at least partially devoted to applauding Rose's own wisdom to set them up, the possibilities that she had had the foresight to understand. Now they just wondered to themselves about what had gone wrong. Thought she wouldn't admit it to Stephen, Laura felt that this was fundamentally unfair. Losing people so often happened naturally; why force it? Jane the blonde and good had believed in exercise, and Stephen had started to run. He thought maybe she should give it a try.

The Borghese wasn't terribly far, but Stephen called a taxi. He'd bought tickets online, for ten in the morning, and he didn't want to be late. Up on the hill, the city looked more like New York's West Village—tidy little buildings with elaborate sconces and handsome flora in the window boxes. Looking at Stephen next to her in the backseat, Laura wondered what his vacation was like, if he was having a good time. She thought he probably was. Maybe she was having a good time too, and just hadn't noticed. That seemed like a nice possibility. Did Stephen think about Jane the blonde and good as much as she thought about John? There was no way to tell. He didn't describe her as blonde and good, but it was what Laura understood. She knew that if the four of them had all been in a room together, breaking the laws of time and space, the original pairings would have prevailed. That was unequivocally true, but it wasn't polite to bring it up. If they were somewhere else, somewhere she'd never been, somewhere where her marriage had never existed, that would have been better. Then she wouldn't be checking for consistency.

Stephen noticed her looking at him and stretched his palm across the seat, open. Laura tucked her hand inside his and let him squeeze. He liked this, feeling like she was going to him, like he had drawn her out. Outside, the leaves in the park rustled noisily—it was high fall, even in Rome, where Laura had believed it always to be summer. Red, orange, yellow—that only happened in New England, she thought, and for about five minutes outside her front door in Brooklyn. Like most things, fall in Rome was more grand, more beautiful. It made her want to stay. New York never felt like this for longer than a few days. It was as though transition—the idea of transition—had set up camp long enough for everyone to get used to what was to come.

The Galleria Borghese had been a palazzo before it became a museum, and it was one of those places, like the Frick in New York, where you immediately wanted to send for your belongings and throw dinner parties and balls for all your friends. As a teenager, Laura liked to go to the Frick and debate with herself over the merits of the various wallpapers, which rooms she would use for her personal chambers, which she would still agree, generously, to share with the public. Most of the time, she would decide the public had enjoyed the house enough, and that it was all for her, thank you very much. John preferred the Guggenheim and had been appalled at her selfishness. He thought public spaces were to be shared. "Yes," Laura explained to him, "that's why it wouldn't be a public space anymore, because I would live there. We could have sixteen cats and a maid and even a suite for your mother, don't you think she'd like that? We could have a chef who only made what we liked to eat, bagels and lox every morning, or blueberry pancakes, whatever we wanted!" John would shake his head, *no, she wasn't serious.* Laura had always hated that about him, his unwillingness to indulge.

The house had pillars and curving staircases and reclining nudes at every turn. The ceilings of the first floor had to be at least twenty feet high—even Stephen was dwarfed by the room's stature. Several tour groups swarmed around them; this one following a woman holding aloft a French flag; this one following a smiley face on a stick. People, fifteen at a time, huddled close around a statue, looking to their leader to decipher the mysteries held within. Laura and Stephen decided to wander aimlessly from one room to the next, stopping here and there to hear what a German docent might say about a particular piece. Neither of them spoke German, but with a pale, luminous David holding up the dripping head of Goliath, and all those guttural sounds, there was little doubt what was being described. Stephen ducked and pulled Laura into the next room, both of them colliding with protruding fanny-packs and elbows the length of the museum.

Laura reached the subsequent room a little out of breath. She was laughing at Stephen, who was in the midst of an impression of a tourist listening raptly to what was being said, staring at the explanatory paper in front of him, and paying no attention at all to the sculpture behind him.

Over his head, there were leaves, marble leaves. When his own attentive audience had stopped listening, Stephen turned to join Laura in looking at what had been behind him, only partially obscured, as it too towered over his head.

Laura followed the leaves down to where they turned into fingers. They turned into strands of hair, long and wavy, like her own. A woman rose out of the earth, still in motion, tree bark beginning to form around her slender, marble legs. Her toes had roots. Behind her, a man was running, so close he had one hand already on her waist, where her skin was covered with marble wood. He was moving quickly, trying so hard to catch her that the fabric he'd been wearing, a sheet, a cloak, had fallen to his waist and was whipping behind him, forever in motion, the soft ends ticked up with an unseen wind. Gray ribbons of regret ran throughout his straining legs, through the leaves, and into her side.

"What is this," Laura asked, not to Stephen, but to anyone.

"Apollo and Daphne," Stephen said. He stood in front of the explanatory placard, his shoulders bent forward to read the small print. "Bernini, 1625. He was only twenty-four."

"What are they doing?" Laura blushed, her voice was too loud for the room. There were other people circling, seeing the scene from all sides. Laura forgot that she did not have roots descending into the basement and the park beneath them, and that she, in fact, could move.

"She's getting away. He's the God of something or other, Light, I think, and he was going to rape her, but she turns into a tree to escape," Stephen said.

Laura felt faint, as though she wanted to sit down, or to walk, but she couldn't. "Like she would do anything to get away, to move on," she said. Stephen came closer. Together, they looked at Daphne's open eyes, at her splayed fingers, each of which had sprouted branches. Apollo's hand, still reaching. "But she didn't quite understand that this is how it would be." Laura felt a hand around her waist, and for a moment imagined it was Apollo, reaching for her, begging her to stay, already knowing in his marble heart that she was gone.

MARJORIE AND THE BIRDS

After her husband died, Marjorie took up hobbies, lots of them, just to see what stuck. She went on a cruise for widows and widowers, which was awful for everyone except the people who hadn't really loved their spouses to begin with. She took up knitting, which made her fingers hurt, and modern dance for seniors, which made the rest of her body hurt, too. Most of all, Marjorie enjoyed birding, which didn't seem like a hobby at all, but like agreeing to be more observant. She'd always been good at paying attention.

She signed up for an introductory course at the Museum of Natural History, sending her check in the mail with a slip of paper wrapped around it. It was the sort of thing that her children made fun of her for, but Marjorie liked to do things properly. The class met twice a week at seven in the morning, always gathering on the Naturalist's Bridge just past the entrance to the park at 77th Street. Marjorie liked that, the consistency. Even on days when she was late—all year, it had only happened twice, and she'd been mortified both times—Marjorie knew just where to find the group, as they always wound around the park on the same path, moving at a snail's pace, a birder's pace, their eyes up in the trees and their hands loosely holding onto the binoculars around their necks.

Dr. Lawrence was in charge. He was a small man, smaller than Marjorie, who stood five foot seven in her walking shoes. His hair was thin but not gone, pale but not white. To Marjorie, he seemed a youthful spirit, though he must have been in his late fifties. Dr. Lawrence had another job at the museum, unrelated to birds. Marjorie could never remember exactly what it was. He dusted off the dinosaurs with a toothbrush, or something. She was too embarrassed to keep asking. But the birds were his real love, that was clear. Marjorie loved listening to Dr. Lawrence describe what he saw in the trees. *Warbling in the fir tree, behind the maple, 11 o'clock. Upper branches, just below the moon. Do you hear them calling to each other? Don't you hear them?* Sometimes Marjorie would close her eyes, even though she knew that wasn't the point. But the park sounded so beautiful to her, like it and she had been asleep together and were only now waking up, were only now beginning to understand what was possible.

Marjorie's husband, Steve, had had a big personality and the kind of booming voice that often made people turn around in restaurants. In the end, it was his heart that stopped working, as they had long suspected it would be. There had been too many decades of three-hour dinners, too much butter, too much fun. Steve had resisted all the diets his doctors suggested on principle—if that was living, what was the point? He'd known that it would happen this way, that he would go down swinging, or swigging as the case may have been. Marjorie understood. It was the children who argued.

Their daughter Kate was the eldest, and already had two children of her own. She would send articles over email, knowing that neither of her parents would read them. Lowering his salt, lowering his sugar, lowering his alcohol intake. Simple exercises that could be done while sitting in a chair—Kate had tried them, they were easy! Marjorie knew how to press delete. She didn't have to listen if she didn't want to.

"It's just that it's so selfish," Kate would say, before her father died. "Doesn't he think about my children? Doesn't he want to know them, to see them grow up?" She lived thirty minutes outside the city, and liked to repeat herself. She always had, even as a child. Kate had two children, a boy and a girl, and they went to the kind of public school one saw in television programs, lily-white and occasionally filled with song. The school was the reason they moved, Kate wasn't shy about saying. "Sometimes parents have to make sacrifices," she said to her mother, who she clearly believed had done no such thing. "Sometimes sacrifices are necessary."

Kate's younger brother lived alone in a derelict apartment building on Amsterdam Avenue, only three blocks from the family homestead. The summer before Steve died, there was some kind of shoot-out in the apartment above Matthew's, a whole family killed. He moved in with his parents for a couple of weeks, and then went back. "What are the odds," he'd said, when Marjorie expressed concern, "of something like that happening twice?" When the children had watched *Peanuts*, Matthew had liked Linus most of all. He had a quality that his teachers always called easy-going, *quiet* in private-school speak, but Marjorie thought he was depressed.

Both kids came over on Sundays, a new tradition fabricated to lessen Marjorie's loneliness. At first, the visits had been helpful, and she'd looked forward to them, especially when there were still papers to sort through and insurance claims to file and bags and bags of clothing to give away. It had been a year and a half, though, since Steve's death, and now Marjorie wasn't sure whom the visits were for.

There was a new doorman, and sometimes he made Matthew call up for permission to enter the building, which made Marjorie feel violently sad, but only for a moment. The apartment was on the sixth floor of a six-floor building on the corner of Central Park West and 83rd Street, and overlooked the park from a series of large windows along the east side of the building. The location had been important to Steve: not the view of the park, which he cared little about, but the view of the lineup for the Macy's Thanksgiving Day Parade, which was unparalleled. Every year, they would have a large viewing party, and everyone would step out on the small wrought-iron balcony, or else press their face to a window. It was an easy way to be popular, and everyone always wanted to be invited back. This year Marjorie had cancelled the party, to the horror of the children, though Kate and her offspring had come anyway. Marjorie had stayed in the bedroom, listening to the radio.

Matthew came up first, holding a plastic bag from a Mexican restaurant on the next block. They were all going to dinner, but Matthew often needed to be fed twice. In his youth, it had seemed charming, as though his appetite for life was too great to fit into standard mealtime portions, but since his thirtieth birthday, all the extra meals had started to gather around his middle. When Marjorie stepped aside to let him in, Matthew made a sheepish face.

"I'm starving," he said. "I haven't eaten all day."

"It's okay," Marjorie said. "Come sit in the kitchen, I'll keep you company."

Matthew looked relieved, and started down the hallway. From behind, he looked like neither Steve nor Marjorie. His dark hair was cut short, so short it poked straight out from his head, a haircut for a simple man. But Matthew wasn't simple, Marjorie thought, just slightly lost. There had been girlfriends now and again, but not for years. Was he in college, the last time there was a girl around? She couldn't remember. He'd always been secretive, and then, after a number of years, there seemed to be nothing to hide. Marjorie knew her son spent a lot of his free time at the small public library a few blocks from his apartment, and that seemed like something normal people did, if they didn't have a lot of money. He had a job she didn't understand, fixing computers for large companies. She hadn't been to his apartment in years, since well before the shooting, but what she remembered of it was that it was both dark and clean. Matthew was fine, he was fine.

They slid into their usual chairs at the kitchen table, Marjorie in back, by the window, and Matthew in front of her, looking out. He peeled back one tinfoil corner and took a bite, which sent a few stray black beans down his chin and onto the table. Marjorie got up and took a plate out of the cupboard, placing it under the burrito. Matthew looked up at her, apologetic.

"Thanks, Mom."

"You're welcome, honey." She sat back down across from him and watched him eat. Marjorie herself was hardly ever hungry anymore—she would have said she ate like a bird, but now she knew that birds weren't actually so delicate. They ripped worms right out of the ground, swallowing them whole. Birds would swoop down and snatch something from each other's mouths. It was violent! She wasn't like that. Without Steve and his oversized appetite, Marjorie hardly ever went to restaurants. Most nights, she would pick at whatever was left in the refrigerator, occasionally summoning the energy to make a fresh batch of soup, or cooking half a chicken breast. It accentuated the loneliness, to cook for one. But it gave her pleasure to watch her son bury his face into something so enormous, what she'd heard him call *super-sized*. That made it sound better than it was. Specks of sour cream now clung to the corners of Matthew's mouth. She thought about getting him a napkin, but didn't. He would wipe the bits away himself, as he always did, with his fingers.

Dr. Lawrence told Marjorie that she was a natural. The trick was to watch for motion with your naked eye, and then to slowly bring your binoculars up without losing sight of the bird. If you had to look down, you'd lose the bird, and just be searching the trees again, square one. Marjorie stayed close to Dr. Lawrence, a few steps behind, and always had her hands at the ready.

"Look, it's a Northern Flicker, do you see? Nine o'clock, just above that big knot. The oak, dead ahead." Dr. Lawrence was capable of standing perfectly still, weight even in his legs. Marjorie thought about asking him if he'd ever done tai chi, but decided not to. He was focused, and she didn't want him to think she was a ditz.

There was a slight breeze in the park, which moved the dappled shade back and forth across the path. Central Park was a wondrous place, and it seemed to be getting bigger. When Marjorie thought about how the park must look from the sky, when the birds were so tired about flying across oceans and over mountains, just for this! To get to her park! She was seized with pride, as though she had planted every tree herself.

"Do you see it, Marjorie?" Dr. Lawrence asked. He was speaking to her directly, but still staring at the bird through his glasses. The other people in the class were a few feet behind, probably trying to find their apartment buildings through the treetops.

The bird had stripes on its back and polka dots on its belly, with a wide black bib around its neck. Marjorie watched as it hopped up and down a branch, investigating something invisible to her eye. "I see it," she said, to Dr. Lawrence, but also to herself. "I see it, I see it." They stood there in silence, motionless, until the bird flew away.

"Whew," Marjorie said. "That was a good one."

Dr. Lawrence turned to her and lowered his binoculars. He had small, frameless glasses, held together with wire so delicate it looked as though he could have made them himself. "I couldn't agree more," he said. Dr. Lawrence spoke in full sentences, not like the people on television, who were always yup-ing and hey-ing each other. Marjorie could have talked to him all day.

There were other people in the class, of course, though as the weeks went on, Marjorie felt as though she and Dr. Lawrence were more and more alone. There were the young women, new mothers in the neighborhood who were looking for a reason to leave the house for an hour. There were the chatty ones in their forties who seemed to be memorizing everything, as if there was going to be a test. There were the women like Marjorie used to be, the ones who filled their days with volunteer jobs and tennis and dates with their grandchildren. She was the oldest one there by five years, maybe even ten. Dr. Lawrence was very generous to put up with her, she thought. But sometimes Marjorie was sure, quite sure, that he enjoyed her company.

Kate had a key, and used it. She came in without announcing herself via the doorman or the doorbell. Kate had the kind of look that nobody questioned; she should have been hired by terrorists. "Mom?" she called from the doorway, "Mom?" Kate was tall, like Steve, with broad shoulders and a no-nonsense haircut that made her look older than she was, boxy around the ears. Matthew had always been the pretty one. Now Marjorie wasn't sure who won that role—it certainly wasn't her. Maybe it was Steve, always smiling so widely in the flattering photographs she'd chosen to keep out.

"Yes, dear, in here," Marjorie said from the living room, trying to make her voice as loud as possible. That was a drawback to living alone that she'd discovered early on. Unused, a voice went all froggy. She often sounded positively amphibian when telemarketers called at seven p.m., having not actually spoken to anyone all day.

She was reading a book about what happened in the park after dark—all the creatures that came out of their hidey-holes, the owls and rats and furry-tailed raccoons. Maybe eventually Marjorie could work up the courage to walk through all by herself at night. Kate would be appalled. Matthew would be worried. She wondered if Dr. Lawrence ever thought about running a night class, a one-off. Maybe she would suggest the idea to him at their next meeting. There might be some insurance issues, she supposed, or some other logistical problem, but he could do it off the books. Scandal! Marjorie loved the thought of cloak-and-dagger. They would meet at the same corner, wearing trench coats. She smiled to herself at the thought of it.

"What's funny? What are you reading?" Kate sat down on the sofa and smoothed out the seat next to her. The sofa looked suddenly shabby, with Kate on it. It had always been just fine, for the last twenty years it had always looked just fine, but now it was all wrong.

Marjorie shut the book, and shook her head. "Oh, nothing." She took off her reading glasses and placed them, folded, in her lap.

If Marjorie had raised the children better, Kate would have said, *it's not nothing, Mom, what are you reading? What just made you laugh? Come on, tell me!* She would have moved closer together and they would have talked for hours about all the birds Marjorie had seen in the park, and how smart Dr. Lawrence was, and how incredible it was to hear a warbler before you saw it and know—not think, but know—exactly what it was. But instead, Kate did just what Marjorie was hoping she wouldn't, and started talking about her day, and how another parent from the school was having an inappropriate relationship with the soccer coach, and she just didn't think it was going to end well. Marjorie did her best to listen, and to be concerned, for of course she did love her daughter very much. There had been times that Marjorie thought she ought to get a pet to serve that purpose, the good listener. When the children were small, Steve had lobbied for a dog, and so they'd had a dog, a great big slobbery one. It had been almost twenty years, though, and Marjorie wasn't sure she was up to another one. She didn't particularly like cats. Maybe she would get a bird, though it now seemed cruel to keep one inside, now that she'd seen them whoop and soar in the park, as high as all that.

It wasn't a crush; that was absurd. Marjorie had been married for fifty-three years. Matthew was the one who used the word first. He'd started coming over on Wednesdays, also. There was a television program he liked, and they sat and watched it together on the new sofa.

"He sounds nice, Mom." Matthew ate entire handfuls of microwaved popcorn at a time, not noticing or caring when kernels fell to the rug. If Marjorie had a bird, the bird would have eaten them. She liked that idea—the bird and her son having a symbiotic relationship.

"Dr. Lawrence is better than nice, he's smart," Marjorie said. The program Matthew liked was about chefs competing for prize money. All the chefs worked very quickly and had tattoos. Marjorie supposed that's what chefs were really like; she'd never known any. She liked the show, seeing behind the scenes. "I go twice a week."

"So, he's like your therapist."

The chefs were making eggs, which Marjorie had never thought was very difficult. But then she saw what they made, the beautiful yolks spilling out onto the judges' plates. The yellow was the exact same color as a canary, with its witchoo-witchoo-witchoo song. Out of nowhere, her eyes felt moist and teary.

"Oh, no," she said. "Don't be silly. What do I need a therapist for? I have you." Marjorie patted her son's knee, and then went into the kitchen to make him more popcorn. Matthew shook his head; she didn't really mean it, not literally, but Marjorie knew it was the kind of thing that would make them both happy, to have it hanging in the air like that.

One Friday morning, Dr. Lawrence brought a paper bag full of fresh bagels for the class. He held it against his chest, and the smell of warm dough filled the air, at least the air closest to Marjorie. She'd just bought a new pair of binoculars, and was looking forward to showing them to Dr. Lawrence. They'd been expensive, but she didn't care. Steve had always shopped that way, with no regard to price tags, but Marjorie had been raised thrifty. The binoculars were her first major purchase since signing up for the class, and she was proud of them. She waited with her arms crossed for Dr. Lawrence to speak. Some of the younger women were still chatting when he cleared his tiny throat, and Marjorie looked sharply at them, on purpose.

"I have some exciting news," Dr. Lawrence said. It was warm, the very end of June. Peak migration was already over, but there were still birds in the trees. Marjorie had learned so much already, and her heartbeat quickened at the notion that there was a new piece of information that Dr. Lawrence was about to impart. "The museum is sending me to the Serengeti desert." He paused, smiling, and looked straight at Marjorie.

"What for?" Marjorie asked, not quite meaning to say it out loud, but not able to stop herself, either.

"To see it!" Dr. Lawrence's pale pink cheeks were brighter than usual—he was excited. Marjorie hadn't seen him look so pleased since they say they saw two downy woodpeckers chomping away on the same tree. "For my backgrounds."

Marjorie remembered then: why was it so hard for her to remember? When Dr. Lawrence wasn't looking at birds, he was painting the backgrounds of the dioramas. He painted the skies and the clouds and the mountains and the brush in the far-off distance.

"Oh," Marjorie said. "How wonderful."

Having received the response he wanted, Dr. Lawrence opened the bag of bagels and passed it around the crowd of people. One woman had brought her baby and had the poor thing strapped to her chest, where her binoculars should have been. Marjorie felt that Dr. Lawrence deserved more than a trip to the desert. He deserved to have someone go with him, someone to go and touch his elbow when she (this person, this other person) saw a bird suddenly streaking across the wide-open sky.

ORIENT POINT

It was August, and the car's air-conditioning was broken. That was part of the problem. John believed in waiting to see if appliances fixed themselves, if some benign magic from the greater universe would intervene. And so there we were, John in front and me in the back with the baby, all the windows down, sweat making the backs of our thighs stick to the seats. It would take three hours to get to his parents' house on the very tip of the North Fork of Long Island, and the open windows only helped when we were moving quickly, which wasn't often the case. John kept looking at us in the rear view mirror—no, not at us, at Eve.

"Is she okay?" He asked. Eve was too small to face forward, and so he could only see the car seat itself in the rearview mirror.

She was damp with sweat, just like us, her tiny brown wisps of hair plastered to her forehead like a doll's molded plastic coif.

"She's fine," I said. "Just hot."

On cue, the baby whimpered. Eve was almost a year old, and had mastered a few consistent words, all of which sounded like a drunk talking in his sleep.

"Sounds like she's hungry," John said. He narrowed his eyes at me. "Is she hungry?"

"She's fine," I said. Even thinking about breast-feeding made my body spring into action. I could feel the internal valves open. She would eat soon enough, whether she was hungry or not. John had made sure of it. Otherwise, we'd arrive at his parents' house, John and Eve slick with sweat, me with sweat and tacky milk.

The day after our wedding, my parents told me they loved John. They said it together, at the kitchen table. I was already five months pregnant.

"He's a good man," my father said. "A good man."

"We're very happy for you," my mother said.

No one thought I would ever get married, not to somebody as clean as John, as fancy. That's what they were really saying—that I'd waddled backwards into it like a scuba driver plopping off the back of a boat. That he wouldn't have married me otherwise, and what luck. And they were right. Eve had three cousins already on her father's side, slim, long children all. There were family outings to the beach, camping trips. They sang songs and did the puzzle. My parents didn't close the door when they used the bathroom, and as far as I knew no one in John's family had ever even had to go.

Eve looked like me, with dark features and a cloudy expression. She often cried when faced with cheery strangers at the grocery store, a trait I admired. She was an excellent screamer. In a few weeks, she would be a year old. I'd always hated it when parents counted in months, the same way that pregnant women counted in weeks, as though their time was too precious to use such large units of measure. John would have described Eve's age in days, if he could count that high. It was like he thought that she was the only baby who had ever been born.

"I am too hot to breathe," I said. We were only forty minutes out of the city but the concrete landscape had already relaxed into long, uninterrupted stretches of trees.

John didn't respond, instead just stared at the road in front of him. We zoomed by the huddled body of a dead deer on the median, and then another. John seemed not to notice.

There was a beach an hour from Orient, one John's parents never went to because people were always nude. We passed the first sign for it on the road and I smacked the back of John's seat.

"Turn here," I said, as though it had been our plan all along. "Turn here turn here turn here." The thought of the water, still cold in August, made my mouth begin to salivate with relief.

He did as he was told. Though he gamely pretended that his parents liked me, John was never in a rush to get me to their house, as white and clean as a furniture showroom. The minute I stepped inside, I could feel the whole family collectively hold their breath. I was an accident, Eve was an accident. We were placeholders that forgot to move on.

Our bathing suits were wadded in somewhere in the duffel bag in the trunk, but when we got out of the car, and I'd unhooked Eve from her seat, the breeze from the ocean felt too good on my skin to wait another minute. "Forget it," I said to John, as he started to unzip the bag. "Just come on."

The path from the small parking lot to the beach itself was a narrow strip of sand carved out of tall sea grass, waving pussy-willows that reached my shoulders. The hot sand poured through the gaps of my flip-flops and stung my toes. Eve made a noise like a wet rag being wrung out, the kind of noise that was ninety percent saliva. John was a yard behind us, his empty hands already clutching at the anxiety of arriving at a beach in his clothes, without a towel.

The beach was empty except for two old women sunning themselves far at the other end. They were too far away for me to tell if they were wearing anything but their sunglasses.

"Hold her for a sec," I said, and passed John the baby. I pulled off my tank top and shorts in less than a minute, peeling the damp cotton of my underwear off too, and dropped all my clothes into a pile on the sand. John stared at me as if I'd grown a third breast. Eve nestled into his chest like a barnacle. "Okay," I said. "I'm going in." And then I walked into the water, the icy Atlantic lapping at my ankles. One by one, I felt each of my blood vessels constrict until my body was half as big as it had been before. I walked until the water came up to my belly-button, and turned around.

John and Eve hadn't moved. They stood static, father and daughter, rock and barnacle, as separate from me as the Atlantic from the Pacific. John and I weren't supposed to have gotten married. We weren't even supposed to have liked each other. We were supposed to have had sex a few times, always high or drunk or both, and then to sheepishly forget each other's names. I would have. There had been possible exits before, choices he'd ignored, but it was still early enough to escape without permanent damage. But it wasn't the two of us that didn't fit, me and Eve. It was only me. John could take Eve and she would be one of them, as comfortable in that pristine white house as he was. She would never spill, never stumble. John would take her; was it strange, that I knew so clearly that he would be the one she clung to? She would see me on holidays, on weekends, and then hardly at all, until she only saw my young face in her baby pictures and recognized the scowl her father had taught her to discard. Everyone would be better off. John would be relieved. His parents would be quietly ecstatic, and never say my name again. I smiled at him from the water before sinking to my knees and letting the cold water rise over my collarbones, over my ears, over my head.

MOHAWK

Camp Mohawk was in the Berkshires, three and a half hours out of the city. Fran and Jim had friends who'd sent their sons, a rowdy lot from the Apthorp, and Fran thought Bobby might benefit from the experience. He was eight, and clung to his mother like a barnacle, only detaching for school and meals. The thought of an entire month with only the two of them in the house struck them as both terribly sad and terribly exciting, and so there they were, zipping up I-95 in the Saab, which creakily gave in to Jim's insistent demands.

Bobby sat in the backseat, and was completely silent until they hit New Haven. Fran kept her hand on the radio tuning knob and switched stations every time a song came on that didn't strike her fancy, which was often.

"What if I don't like anyone there?" Bobby said. He stared out the window, as though the answer waited in a passing Connecticut gas station.

"Oh, honey!" Fran swiveled around in her seat and gripped the head rest, peeking through. "Of course you will! And they'll all like you!" The camp was for boys who favored the outdoors, with canoe trips and hikes on the Appalachian Trail. They'd packed ten pairs of underwear, ten pairs of socks, four pairs of pants, four pairs of short, eight T-shirts, two sweatshirts, one mess kit and one canteen, all with Bobby's name emblazoned in one place or another. Jim would have been worried, too.

"Okay," he said, still unconvinced. Fran handed him a Snickers bar, his last piece of candy for four weeks. Bobby took it with both hands and didn't ask any more questions.

All the boys were split into bunks based on their age; as one of the youngest in the camp, Bobby was a Scout. He seemed to take this designation seriously, and nodded at his two slim-hipped counselors, who both looked so much like children that Jim half wanted to steal Bobby away, throw him in the back of the car, and drive away as quickly as possible. Franny eyed them both with particular interest, and the boys blushed under her gaze. She'd worn heels and lipstick even knowing full well that she would have a tour of the grounds before leaving them her only child.

"Amherst," she said to one of the counselors. "How *fabulous.*"

The bunk itself was a giant tent on a wooden platform, with twelve cots. It reminded Jim of movies about Vietnam. The bathroom, shared by several bunks, was a short walk up a hill. This was why they'd included flashlights on the pre-camp shopping list. The Amherst boy saw the look in Jim's eye and started gibbering on about the buddy system, as earnest as if he'd invented it. "Fine," Jim said. "Sounds fine." He put Bobby's trunk at the foot of his bed.

By the time they left, Bobby had already found three boys

from his school, and was talking with great excitement about a bear that had been seen in the area. The counselors told all parents not to say goodbye just before they drove away, but to skulk off as if they were going to the movies and leaving him with a new babysitter. Franny couldn't resist blowing kisses, and Jim honked twice, as though the horn could say everything that he wanted to. When they saw Bobby wave in the rear-view mirror, Franny cried, but only for a few minutes, and then she was back to playing with the radio.

"It is far," she said. "Maybe we should have some lunch. Emily Dickinson? She had to eat, right?" She found a station playing the Beach Boys and sat back, crossing her arms over her chest.

The main drag in Northampton was lined with shops selling handmade dreamcatchers and incense sticks. Grown women wore tie-dye. On a traffic island, a man played a tuba and bubbles came out. It was everything Jim had never liked about summer camp, all in one town. Fran was in heaven.

"Dorothy, we're not in Kansas anymore," Jim said.

"Dorothy, we were never in Kansas," Franny said back.

It was already two-thirty, and most places were closed for lunch. There was a diner that served breakfast all day, and it seemed like the best they could hope for. Fran and Jim slid into a vinyl booth at the far end of the room, several tables away from the nearest patrons. She opened the tri-fold laminated menu and propped it up on the table in front of her.

"A grinder is a hoagie is a slider is a sub, yes?" she asked.

"Something like that." The room smelled like bacon and

orange juice, not unpleasantly.

A waitress in a red-and-white gingham apron sauntered over. She was chewing gum. Fran ordered a short stack of pancakes with whipped cream on top, and made a sheepish face, as thought she really shouldn't have, all for the waitress' benefit. Jim ordered wheat toast and some fruit, and even before the words were out of his mouth, Fran was fuming.

"Thanks," she said, as soon as the waitress had vanished into the kitchen. "Now I look like a pig."

"She's a waitress at a diner, Fran," Jim said. "I think people have ordered pancakes before."

"You just always have to do that, don't you?" She glared at him.

When the waitress came back with their coffees, Fran turned her head the opposite direction, like a pouting child who refused to eat its pureed vegetables. Jim thanked the waitress twice for good measure.

"So," Jim said, imagining the remaining three hours of the drive home, "you think he'll be okay?" Bobby was the kind of boys other boys always adored, and thrived when he got to disappear into a group of his peers, like a dog. Jim knew he'd be fine, but wanted to hear Franny say it.

"Sure," Franny said. She looked at Jim as though summer camp had been his idea. "God, the house is going to be so empty." She stared into her coffee cup.

Jim tried to remember what they'd done with their time before Bobby was born, how they'd spent our evenings. There had been more drinking. If they weren't doing fractions or sounding out three-syllable words, who were they? But Jim resented the implication that without Bobby there, they'd be limping through the summer, always feeling the acute loss of their parental selves. It was not as though they had nothing to talk about. There was something, though, behind her worry. Jim watched her swirl her sludgey coffee, swishing it one way, than the other.

"I'll be there."

Fran raised an eyebrow, and put the cup back down on the formica. A few drops of coffee slipped over the side of the mug and drew an archipelago across the speckled white surface. She wiped it up with her paper napkin. "So will I."

Not only could Jim not remember our life before Bobby, he couldn't remember a single conversation they'd ever had. It was as though they'd both been replaced by actors, a man and a woman who were choosing their roles anew. Jim looked at his wife and saw her familiar face, the curve of her cheeks and the exclamation point of her chin. She could have been sitting across from anyone. There was no hazy affection floating over the table, or between their feet.

"Let's just eat and go," she said, as the pancakes arrived, three fluffy ones the size of the plate. Fran poured maple syrup back and forth, back and forth, making a softened grid out of the liquid sugar. "Okay?"

"Okay," Jim said, and did what he was told.

They got back in the car a few minutes after three. Jim drove, and Franny kept the map open on her lap, as though they would need it. Jim saw her out of the corner of his eyes, fingering routes to places they weren't going. The mountains of North Carolina. The Oregon coastline. Las Vegas. If Jim had taken a right and started driving there, Franny wouldn't have noticed until they hit the desert: why not? There was no one waiting for them at home. Still, he kept straight and let the highway unfold in front of him. Over their heads, the sky was unseasonably gray, and Jim had to struggle to keep his eyes open. He drove for an hour before Franny announced that she had to pee. They were in Hartford, a city whose skyline seemed to consist only of smokestacks and abandoned office buildings. Jim pulled into a gas station, and sat in the car while Franny scampered inside. He was happy for the break.

They'd talked about having more children before. When Bobby was small, teetering around the house on his tiny legs like Frankenstein's monster, it seemed like the natural thing to do. Siblings were healthy; everyone said so. Even though Franny didn't have any, and Jim didn't particularly like his, a sister or a brother still conjured up images of Christmas trees and endless games of War. Bobby would be better for it. But that was before Fran was going to exercise class, before she'd gone back to work. Before Jim knew it, Bobby was three, then four, then five. Now he was eight, and Franny looked at Jim like a felon whenever he brought it up.

It was starting to rain. Small drops hit the top of the windshield and scattered, forming intricate pathways to the hood of the car. Franny pulled the latch and leapt inside as quickly as if she was being chased. She slammed the door and shook her head like a wet dog.

"It's just water," Jim said.

"Please." She was annoyed by the rain, and doubly annoyed

by him. "You know about my hair."

Instead of turning the key in the ignition, Jim put his hands on the wheel and watched the streams rush and intersect on the windshield. Was it raining at Camp Mohawk, too? Bobby's yellow rain jacket was folded in his trunk, along the left side. Jim hoped he knew where to find it, or that one of his counselors would be there to help if he couldn't. He was only eight. Now that he wasn't in the car, eight seemed young, far too young to spend an entire month without his parents. If he had a brother, they could have gone together, always stopping to tie each other's shoes.

"I think we should have another kid," Jim said. "I really think we should have another kid."

Fran looked at him like he was from Mars, or somewhere even less habitable. "Right now?" She gestured to the small back seat of the car. "I don't think there's room."

"I'm serious, Franny."

"Well, so am I!" There were drops of rain suspended in her hair, tiny perfect orbs of water. She leaned against the seat and closed her eyes.

The house could easily hold another child. It could hold three more! There would be noise on the staircase and shouts and crashes. Bobby would be the grand marshal of the parade. Jim looked at Fran's closed eyes and saw that she was right to wonder what they would do when they were all alone. If he'd suggested turning around and driving back to the camp, Jim knew she would have agreed. They sat in the parking lot of the gas station until the rain let up, both silently plotting their exit routes. Both had put in enough time. If they weren't going forward, Jim refused to tread water indefinitely. He opened his mouth, as if the rain would crack open the glass and land on his tongue, cold and dark, like mercury. When Jim started the car, he didn't care where they were going, just that they would get there quickly.

HOT SPRINGS ETERNAL

The vacation was Teddy's idea: see the West! If you asked Richard, driving across deserts and mountains in the middle of the summer sounded more like punishment than a reward, but Teddy was exuberant, and that could be convincing. Richard thought that if he put it off, and waited until just the month before to say yay or nay, Teddy would give up, as he often did, and they could spend the summer dashing across the city from air-conditioned room to air-conditioned room. Instead, when the semester was over, and all of Richard's grades were in, with the students' papers marked and duly returned, Teddy pulled a gigantic, messy burrito of a file folder out from under their bed. Tiny newspaper clippings slipped out onto their duvet. Richard worried about the smudgy ink against the white cotton, but let it happen anyway. He could clean up when Teddy, distracted, left the room.

"How have I not vacuumed that up?" Richard asked.

"You only vacuum on Thursdays," Teddy said. "On Thursdays, it lives in my closet." He tittered, so pleased.

New York was bad in the heart of the summer; that was true. Richard could trade stickiness for scenery. They'd fly into

Denver and rent a car, head towards the Pacific. Teddy's idea of a good time was pulling off the highway every so often to look at giant manmade objects: balls of twine, plaster dinosaurs, diners shaped like hot dogs. He'd grown up in Ocala, Florida, which had given him a taste for the bizarre, that and the need to add sugar to most beverages. The rental car was small and boxy, Japanese. Teddy liked to say "Arigato" to parking garage attendants and teenage girls working drive-thru windows, but still complained they weren't driving something larger, more imposing.

"Like a pick-up truck?" Richard had asked.

"Ooh," Teddy said. "Yes, please." He mimed a giant steering wheel, and careened off the road. Most of the time, Teddy drove on the passenger's side, an open map ignored in his lap.

"Do you know how much gas it takes to fill up a truck?" Richard said.

"Killjoy." Teddy was younger by five years, still in his early thirties. When they met, Richard had been an older man. Somehow, though, no matter how much older Richard got, Teddy never seemed to age. Every year at Richard's birthday party, which Teddy invariably had thrown, he would cover his ears and shriek at the number, as though such a thing could never, never come for him.

Richard's therapist, Robin, was a large woman—not merely heavyset, pleasantly plump, but so big she spilled out of her normal-sized office chair in several different directions. She reminded Richard of Edna Turnblad from *Hairspray*—Divine, not John Travolta. This was one of the things he liked best about her. Richard didn't spill, exactly, but he was what Teddy affectionately called "schlubby," and he was soft everywhere one could be soft, right down to the wispy brown hairs still clinging to his hairline. Richard had been proud when the word came out of Teddy's lapsed Catholic mouth—a win for the Jews.

Robin believed in Jesus, which Richard knew from various objects in the office and on her person—a cross here, a cross there. She also seemed to believe that Richard and Teddy could make it work, which Richard chalked up to the fact that Robin had never actually met Teddy, and was picturing someone far more suitable. She was interested in success. During their sessions, Robin and Richard talked about ways he could stop condescending to Teddy, which she seemed to think was a problem.

"And your last fight?" Robin sat at a desk, which Richard liked. It made the whole thing seem more official, less touchy-feely. These were real problems—why should he be on a couch? During every session, Robin demolished an impressively large bottle of Mountain Dew. She used a straw, which had something to do with her tooth enamel. Richard had asked.

"Oh, you know, more of the same." Richard thought about ways to make himself sound less insensitive, less harsh. Teddy was the better looking of the two; that had always been the case, and still was. He had a rakish quality, with slightly wild eyes and hair that seemed to betray Teddy's usual state of excitement. Was it so awful that Richard had noticed the growing belly, the softer cheeks, when Richard himself had always possessed such things?

"Yesterday, I was telling him about one of my students, and right in the middle of the conversation, he looks at me and says, 'You didn't tell me I looked cute today.' And then he made a pouty face! Right in the middle of what I was talking about."

"Uh-huh." Robin's face was impassive—all white, all clear. Her dark brown hair hung straight to her shoulders, curving out slightly to accommodate her cheeks. She nodded, which Richard knew didn't mean she agreed with what he was saying.

Here was the goal: see the country. New York was always the same. Los Angeles, San Francisco, Boston. There were the same boutique hotels, the same shops, the same museums. Richard and Teddy were looking for the parts in between. It was either this or go on a gay cruise, and Richard had some pride, after all. He hadn't driven so much since he was a teenager on Long Island, and the wheel felt good in his hands, the pedal familiar under his foot. Teddy cheered every time they crossed a county line, sometimes giving Richard's bicep a little squeeze. They made it out of the city in less time than expected.

Motels with flashing vacancy signs lined the main drag of Glenwood Springs. The springs themselves were the reasons that Teddy wanted to stop. He read aloud, rapturously, using his finger to guide his eye across the small type. "*Featuring the world's largest outdoor mineral hot springs pool, this touristy town offers innumerable activities, both for the active traveler and those in search of relaxation….*" Richard scanned the shops and bars and gleaming new chain stores. Colorado didn't look that different from Long Island, if you took the mountains and rivers away.

According to the guidebook, the natural hot springs were what drew Doc Holliday to the town, where he eventually died. "I guess he wasn't really a doctor after all, if he thought some boiling hot, rotten egg bathwater was going to make him feel better," Teddy said, then snorted quietly. Teddy had always been adept at amusing himself, which Richard liked. He was excellent at dinner parties, no matter who he was sitting next to. "Ooh! Look at that one!" He pointed out the window and wiggled in his seat, sending the guidebook and an already crumpled map of the United States to the floor of the car.

Richard was not surprised at Teddy's choice. In their previous travels, Teddy had never once wanted to stay at a Holiday Inn or a Marriott, places where you could count on clean sheets and the comforting smell of bleach in the bathroom. Instead, he liked the hotels that looked on the verge of destruction, with words spelled incorrectly, or ones that looked like cottages where Snow White or the Swiss Miss might work at the front desk. Teddy's finger now pointed at a small motel with two stories and external staircases. The entire structure was painted sea-foam green, with plastic mermaids and seashells affixed to the walls in a haphazard fashion. It reminded Richard of his dead grandmother's living room on the Jersey shore.

"Honey, they think we're at the beach. How can we disappoint them?" Teddy knit his fingers together, as if in prayer. Behind him, a mermaid peeked out from behind her molded plastic hair. Richard turned the wheel and pulled into the parking lot of The Seashore Inn…The Mountains. "Come on, baby," Teddy said, nuzzling against Richard's cheek as they took the bags out of the trunk. "You've got to love those dots."

"Ellipses," Richard said. "They're ellipses."

The inside of the office looked alarmingly normal—no sand, no ambient sounds of lapping waves. A young woman with icy blonde hair waited expectantly for them to approach the counter.

"Hello," Richard said, reading the woman's nametag. "Inga. Are there a lot of Ingas in Colorado?"

She smiled generously. If her hair hadn't been pulled back so tightly, Inga might have looked like a wide-faced version of one of the motel's resident fish-women. "I am from Sweden," she said, bowing her head slightly. Teddy bowed back, lowering his torso until it was perpendicular to the floor. He'd been a dancer once upon a time, and Richard knew those impulses were hard to contain. Whenever they stood on the street corner, waiting to cross, Teddy's feet would turn out to first position, which he swore was unconscious. Some of Teddy's former lovers had been dancers, too, and whenever they ran into each other on the street, Richard imagined an elaborate, naked pas de deux. Certain things he had to let slide.

Inga-from-Sweden gave them the keys to Room 105, and momentarily vanished into the depths of the office.

"Oh, God, Richard, look," Teddy nudged him in the shoulder. "They're ranked." On the wall behind the desk, The Seashore Inn proudly displayed its AAA single diamond rating, given every year from 1984 through 1989.

"'Tis better to have loved and lost…" Richard said, shaking his head. Inga-from-Sweden reappeared, the apples of her cheeks rosier than before. She thought Teddy was handsome, Richard could tell. He'd seen it before. Women always liked Teddy; they tried to make him their best new girlfriend.

"So," Teddy said, sidling up to the counter and sticking out his bottom like a teenaged girl. "What's the deal with the hot springs?" He was cute, that was for sure. Richard could deny lots of things about Teddy, but not that. Teddy turned towards Richard and smiled. There were times when Richard was sure Teddy could hear his thoughts. It was strangely comforting.

Inga-from-Sweden told them to wait until after nine o'clock to hit the springs, when the rate would be discounted to seven dollars apiece—nobody needed more than an hour in there, anyway, she said. Richard stretched out on the bed in his swimsuit with his own, imported pillow behind his head. Teddy stood, nude, at the foot of the bed, and recited their dining options from the guidebook.

"*O'Kay's Cattle Ranch—Riverfront dining in the heart of town. Expect plenty of crowds in season, but Colorado-sized portions and a full bar.* Wonder if they have a mechanical bull. Don't you think someone in this town probably has a mechanical bull?" Teddy raised one arm over head and did a little giddy-up, sending his tummy and lower bits into a jiggle.

"What else." Richard covered his eyes with his forearm. Slivers of the green walls peeked through, along with flashes of Teddy's rear end as he paced back and forth across the carpet.

"*Maria's Cantina—As authentic as you can get this far from the border. Wandering mariachi...*okay, no way. *Lemming's*

New York Diner? Are they serious? Oh, God, Richard, let's go get some pastrami. Who do these people think they are? What do they use to make their bagels, rotten egg water?" Sometimes, when he was excited, his barely Southern accent became more pronounced. Teddy had lived in New York for ten years, and with Richard in Chelsea for five. In no way was he in any position to question the presence of pastrami on a menu in Colorado. Nonetheless, Richard acquiesced. On the map, the diner seemed to be a short walk from the hot springs, and Richard wanted red meat. What was the point of being in the middle of the county if you couldn't eat a local cow? Surely that marbled flesh wouldn't have traveled too far.

Lemming's New York Diner was inside the lobby of another hotel, just across the street from O'Kay's Cattle Ranch, which seemed to have more screaming five-year-olds than cowboys, judging from the scene through the restaurant's picture window. The walls at Lemming's were lined with subway tiles, and each table was a stop of its own, as signified by a sign overhead. Richard and Teddy were 14th Street, not far from home.

A waitress appeared. She was wearing an apron with a sea of bagels, or mountains of bagels, depending on your perspective. Her name was Nadia, and she had a voice like a linebacker. Teddy's eyes flew open, enthralled. They ordered pastrami and roast beef sandwiches, and potato pancakes on the side, with both applesauce and sour cream. Two cream sodas. One banana split.

"It's like having Marlene Dietrich ask you if you want

lettuce and tomato," he hissed across the table, after she had gone.

"They call the borscht 'beet soup,'" Richard said.

"Well, isn't that what it is?" Teddy didn't look up from the plastic menu.

"I guess." Richard watched as a small replica of a subway car rattled around the restaurant ceiling. Tiny people stared out, justifiably alarmed that they'd never reach their destination.

Glenwood Springs' actual hot springs were owned and operated by the largest and most expensive hotel in town. Teddy rattled off figures from the book: *Each year, more than two million people dip their toes in the naturally warm water— some for relaxation, some for healing, some for the smell!*

"It does not say that." Richard pulled his wallet out of his back pocket as they approached the entrance, which sloped down towards the basement of the hotel—it was like a water park, with gleaming turnstiles and a damp, slippery floor.

Teddy laughed, and then sniffed the air. "It's not that bad, really."

A dark-haired boy in his twenties manned the cash register. "Just wait." He too had a heavy accent, which made his jaw sound as though it weighed fifty pounds. "*Jah-st way-ate.*"

Teddy raised an eyebrow. "Where are you from?"

"Czech Republic. You know Praha?" The boy was maybe twenty-one. He looked like one of Richard's students, like any of Richard's students. His hair fell in a low swoop over his forehead. The boy hopped down off his wooden stool and bent over to reach a stack of thin, well-worn towels.

"Is your name really Bill?" Everyone under the age of thirty in the entire town seemed to have a nametag and a voice that moved like molasses. Bill's nametag was pinned to the back pocket of his jeans.

"Yah, like Billy the Kid?" Bill smiled a sideways smile, first at Teddy, and then, after a moment, at Richard. "Don't stay in hot tub too long." He took another moment to drink them in, to see if he had judged right. "Party tonight at hostel, on Grand Av-noo." He slid their towels across the counter, and then reached down and grabbed two more, and piled them on top. "Extra," Billy the Kid said. "For friends." Richard thought he saw Teddy's tongue snake across his lower lip.

The slick floor led through the basement of the hotel, past changing rooms and lockers. Armed with their extra towels, Teddy followed Richard through the swinging doors, out to the pool.

The scene reminded Richard of a nightclub, the kind of place he'd spent his adult life trying to avoid; the kind of place with go-go boys standing on pedestals, dancing in nothing but their underwear. It was the energy of the place, the thick cloud of steam over the surface of the water, all the people, people, people. Richard turned around to find Teddy's mouth open.

"Come on, you," Richard said. Plastic lounge chairs with colorful towels draped over them lined the pool, which stretched all the way back towards the mountains. "Let's get smelly."

The truth was, though, that the smelliness had subsided. Even though the air was warm, now down to the mid-70s, the water was warmer, and looked inviting. They found unoccupied chairs halfway down one side of the pool, which stretched on interminably, bigger than Olympic-sized. Over their heads, dark, craggy outlines of mountains loomed and seemed far away. The sky was all that was above them.

"Shall we?" Richard asked, but Teddy was already jogging on the pads of his feet towards the shallow steps.

The pool was jammed. At the shallow end, by Teddy's wet calves, a boy in water wings paddled on his stomach. Richard took a step into the water, and felt the warmth close around his left ankle, and then his right. He couldn't imagine coming in the daytime, what that would be like. It seemed appropriate to submerge oneself in the darkness, as if floating through the giant, open sky. He let the water take him, inch by inch. A body's length ahead, Teddy was already on his back with his arms outstretched, oblivious to the crowds walking heavily and slowly swimming around his prostrate form.

The small boy's father appeared when Richard was up to his bellybutton, the water swishing in and out like an overflowing drain. Richard's body had never been taut—fit, perhaps, at various points—but never precisely taut. The boy's father was just that; it must have made for an easier canvas. Tattooed across his ribcage, there was a six-inch portrait of the Bride of Frankenstein, her hair standing justifiably on end. The man leaned down to scoop up his son, and as he carried him off, feet kicking and splashing, Richard saw Frankenstein's monster himself on the man's other side—the couple separated forever by his lungs.

Teddy floated closer, using his hands as oars. "Let's move

here," he said. "I want to live in the rotten eggs." His wet hair waved under the surface, electric.

"You got it, sister." Richard took Teddy's feet in his hands and plunged forward, sending them both towards the deep end.

It had taken Richard exactly three months to tell Robin what the problem was. He'd spent his first dozen sessions calmly describing his issues with University hierarchy, the Bush administration, and his younger sister's manic procreation. But Teddy was always there, lurking quietly in the back of his throat, somewhere near his uvula.

"There is this one thing," Richard started. It had to do with Florida, and sugar, and Teddy's mother. Robin nodded. The window behind her looked out onto 22nd Street, and Richard could see people's heads bobbing along as they walked their dogs and talked on the phone. He'd had other boyfriends before, though nothing as serious, and certainly nothing as long. He thought about how funny it would be to see one of them walk by, just then, how he could take that as a sign, and run out the door, winding up in someone's unsuspecting arms. Oh, the thrill! In Richard's life, there seemed to be no cinematic flourish. Maybe that's what he was missing. Maybe that's what they had on the open road. "He's not, I don't know, worldly." Teddy, on the other hand, had had a string of boyfriends: actors, the other dancers, limber, elegant smokers. All of Teddy's friends had probably laughed when he first introduced them to Richard. They had probably guffawed. He probably reminded them of their parents.

"Worldly?" Robin had no doubt learned this trick on her first day of therapist school. She was excellent at repeating back key words and phrases. She took a slurp of Mountain Dew, and crossed her arms over her stomach, clutching her turkey-leg forearms.

"He never wants to go to Paris, or go to the symphony, or read poems." Richard looked at the spines of the books of Robin's shelves, the cross around her neck. There was a gurgle in his stomach. He wondered what kind of books Robin read in her spare time, if she read at all. He couldn't imagine her doing the crossword puzzle, or playing Scrabble, or leaping out of her chair to let a poem spill from her lips. He knew what she was going to say.

"And how do you feel about that?"

"I feel like I'm always the one pushing us to do the things I want to do. It would be nice to have him just do them, you know, without my having to ask." Richard closed his eyes for a minute. Sometimes he and Robin did that together, at the end of their sessions. At first, he thought she was insane, and only did it to humor her. Now he closed his eyes at the drop of a hat: on the subway platform, at the dinner table, in bed. Robin called it "taking stock." Richard called it "the no Teddy zone," but only to himself. Sometimes Richard would open his eyes and find Teddy staring at him, mystified.

"And how do you say that?" Robin's legs were crossed at the ankle. Her sandals were beige, like the carpet. Everything in her office was as neutral as possible. Richard liked that about her; she had chosen to choose nothing personal.

"What do you mean? I tell him exactly that, that it wouldn't kill him to think about someone else for a change. That after five years, he should know what day the garbage goes out, and to send my sister's kids birthday cards every year and not just when he feels like it." Richard took a tissue out of the box on Robin's desk and ripped it into tiny little pieces.

Teddy was a crier. He cried at television programs, and intermittently during his daily phone calls with his mother. This had alarmed Richard in the beginning of their relationship, but he'd gotten used to it. On the sliding scale of bodily functions, it was something like a sneeze. The major problem was that Teddy left used tissues in every room of the house, tissues which Richard would then have to pick up and throw away. It also meant that no matter who had started the argument, or who was at fault, Richard would end up apologizing.

"Uh-huh," Robin said. "I see."

On the opposite edge of the pool, several older ladies in bathing caps sat in what looked like something out of an S&M club. Shallow chaise lounges made out of metal tubes sat some ten inches beneath the surface of the pool, where bathers could experience all the pleasure of the hot springs without the bother of physical exertion. Richard and Teddy watched, only their faces out of the water, while one of the ladies rose, dripping, from the pool and shuffled around to the back of her chair, where she popped in a quarter. A moment later, bubbles erupted in her empty chair, turning the area into a one-person Jacuzzi.

"Oh, my God," Teddy said. "Me next." He held Richard's

hand under water, and for a moment, when Teddy's long fingers closed around his fist, Richard was in love, just like that. They treaded water, their shorts ballooning upward, and waited for a turn. Across the pool, a young couple swam by, their eyes masked by large, square goggles. The girl paused to readjust her bathing suit, and after giving her strap a tug, swam up to her boyfriend's face and gave him a kiss. Their goggles bumped together. It was like a commercial for the place: Love in the Time of Sulpher.

Teddy had to pee, and scooted over to a staircase. He had a funny, slightly ducky walk, another remnant from his days as a dancer, more side-to-side than up-and-down, and it was even sillier when he was dripping wet in his slightly-too-small bathing trunks. Had his stomach ever looked that way before? Richard stayed put and watched the ladies' feet bob under the surface. One of them closed their eyes, and so he did, too. He pictured Robin's office filled with water. There was a breeze coming from the mountains, blowing down the river that was directly behind the hotel. His face was cool, and dark. In Richard's imagination, he was so dark that he was invisible. When Teddy came back, splashing loudly, he was smiling.

"Billy the Kid is going to come over later," he said, and took a hit off an imaginary joint. "Before the party."

"You really want to go to that? A party full of kids?" Richard was old; he sounded old. But he couldn't help it. He was their teacher, not their friend. They wouldn't have invited him without Teddy; without Teddy, he wouldn't have gone. It was obvious.

"Well, yeah." Teddy looked offended. "Why, you don't? It's like Epcot Center, kids get sent here from all over. It's going to be fun." He ran a hand across his head, slicking his hair back into a short paintbrush. He hadn't shaved in a few days, and the stubble was starting to turn into something slightly angry.

"What if, after this, we walked up to Doc Holliday's grave? It's just a few blocks from the Seashore. Isn't that more fun than going to a party with a bunch of kids?" Richard straightened his legs, and half his body rose out of the water. Steam came off his skin. If he were a woman, people would ask if he was pregnant. If he were a woman, people would ask if he was Teddy's mother. The five years between them had stretched into ten or fifteen. Still under the water up to his neck, Teddy rolled his eyes. "Of course you'd say that."

One of the old ladies' bubbles were up. Teddy scrambled into the empty chair, and popped a quarter into the machine, leaving Richard steaming alone.

"Five minutes," Teddy said, with ten feet of pool between them. "Let's talk about it in five minutes." He closed his eyes.

They stayed until the pool closed, and someone—Billy the Kid, maybe—shut all the lights off, and only the stars perked up the inky sky.

When Teddy decided to move in, he did it all at once, not gradually, like their friends' boyfriends, who seemed to move one article of clothing at a time. Teddy and his U-Haul blocked traffic on 24th Street for an hour and a half, during which time he made Richard stand in front, apologizing to motorists. Richard had found the whole thing very romantic.

Teddy didn't care about pissing people off, he just wanted to move in as quickly as possible; their love was that important. Or at least that's what Richard thought at the time. It turned out later that the van was a loaner from work and needed to be back after lunch. Still, Richard loved to picture Teddy breathlessly running up and down the stairs holding a lamp, a suitcase, a stack of loose papers from his desk. The honking horns and angry cabdrivers were all just part of the scenery. Richard never closed his eyes then, not even when they kissed.

Only when they were out of the pool did the smell begin to multiply, to cover every inch of their skin. Richard wrapped a towel around his chest, all the way up to his armpits, before putting his shorts back on.

"So, are we going to walk up to the cemetery? Do you want to?" Richard was thinking positively. If he sounded relaxed, then Teddy would react more favorably.

"What? No, we're going to the party. I already told Billy." Teddy's face turned hard. He looked like a clay statue, still wet. There was more to cut away.

"Teddy, come on. You don't really want to go. Don't be stupid." Richard knew instantly that this was a mistake.

"No, Richard, *you* don't want to go. And you know what, you don't have to." Teddy had a towel wrapped loosely around his wet bathing suit, and when the towel dropped to the ground, he didn't stop to pick it up. He just kept walking. Richard stopped and let him go, watching his shirtless upper half move side to side, side to side, until he turned the corner at the end of the block, and was gone.

Robin said that Richard would have to decide, that she couldn't decide for him. There were a number of things that Richard knew Teddy loved about him—stability and responsibility chief among them. He gave practical gifts. He did not believe in three-ways. He believed in taking out the garbage. These were not exciting features. And what did Richard love about Teddy? If Richard was the earth, Teddy was the sky. If the room was beige, then Richard was beige. Teddy couldn't be beige if his life depended on it. Instead of stupid, the word 'carefree.' The word 'open-minded.' The word 'romantic.' If he tried to phrase it for someone else, the vocabulary came more readily to his tongue.

Richard walked the three blocks down Grand Avenue towards the hostel. He wanted to go to Doc Holliday's grave and pull a gun out of the ground. He wanted to send all the beautiful boys and girls back to their respective countries. He wanted to widen his stance and stomp in and terrify everyone with his presence. He thought, maybe if they'd gone to the grave, maybe Teddy would have said something so brilliant, and so thoughtful, that he'd never have to wonder again. He pictured Robin standing at the gates to the cemetery, cheering him on like he was finishing a marathon, headstones streaming by him in streaks of silver and gold.

The Glenwood Springs Hostel was in a one-story yellow house. There was a hand-painted sign with a bright sun in the upper left-hand corner. Faded Tibetan prayer flags ran the length of the porch, and hung low enough that Richard had to stoop to get to the front door. A kayak leaned lazily against the wall, as if pointing the way.

Inga-from-Sweden was off duty, and manning the makeshift bar in the entrance-way, and chatting with two dread-locked teenagers in patchwork pants. She waved at Richard, who gave a weak wave back. Inga was the kind of girl who'd wave at anyone. She was still wearing her nametag. Without being asked, she nodded in the direction of a doorway. Other people's boyfriends had done this before.

Teddy was in the living room, nestled into a deep, stained couch, his legs tucked up beneath him like a child. He was wearing someone else's T-shirt, and it pulled across his chest. Richard pictured Teddy walking in, wet and stinking, and wanted to cry. Billy the Kid sat next to Teddy on the couch, too close. They were laughing. In a funny way, they reminded Richard of the way he and Teddy must have looked when they met, only with Teddy playing Richard's part—older, wiser, broader.

"Theodore," Richard started.

Teddy looked up. It didn't matter that he'd been laughing—when he saw Richard, his eyes were wet. "You came," he said. Richard could see it, suddenly, that Teddy was too old for this too, that he had been coming along, slowly, a step behind Richard. He was wearing someone else's T-shirt. Who lived in this place? Richard took a step forward, and then paused. There were other people in the room—not Marlene Dietrich, but girls like her, girls with low voices, and boys, God, the young, beautiful boys. It didn't matter. None of them mattered. Teddy sat up straight, eyes locked on Richard's.

"Here," Richard said, peeling off his own damp T-shirt,

the pale expanse of his belly now exposed. He wanted Teddy back; he was sure. Richard held his shirt out in the palm of his hand. "Put this on."

ACKNOWLEDGMENTS

Thanks to my classmates and professors from the University of Wisconsin-Madison's MFA program: Samar Fitzgerald, Emma Snyder, Phil Sandick, Nate Brown, Ben Thompson, Jesse Lee Kercheval, Judy Mitchell, and Lorrie Moore.

Thanks to the Wisconsin Institute for Creative Writing for the Halls Emerging Artist Fellowship, which allowed me to stay in Madison and write for another year. Thanks also to Ron Wallace, Ron Kuka, Amy Quan Barry, and Amaud Johnson for their always entertaining company.

Thanks to my patient and kind readers: Edan Lepucki, Stuart Nadler, Ariel Djanikian, Rae Meadows, Alex Darrow, Thomas Yagoda, Dan Chaon, Alyssa Knickerbocker, Antonia Fusco, and Sophie Rosenblum.

Thanks to David Gutowski, Jami Attenberg, Kevin Brockmeier, Lauren Cerand, Caitlin Roper, and Maud Newton for being inclusive and encouraging.

Thanks to the best, smartest, cheerleaders ever: Julie Klam, Jennifer Gilmore, Bethanne Patrick, Elliott Holt, Emily Mandel, Alexander Chee, Allison Devers, Patrick Brown, Jennifer Pooley, Bindu Wiles, Hyatt Bass, Stephanie Anderson, Shya Scanlon, Michele Filgate, Kathleen Nolan, Melissa Klug, Joe Wallace, and the rest of the Virtuous Circle.

Thanks to Mary Gannett, Zack Zook, Henry Zook, and the entire, dazzling staff of BookCourt.

Thanks to Flatmancrooked, whose staff has championed me more than anyone I'm not related to: Elijah Jenkins, Deena Drewis, and Kaelan Smith.

Thanks to Stephin Merritt, Claudia Gonson, Sam Davol, John Woo, and Shirley Simms, for hiring a roadie who can't carry much.

Thanks to my friends: Ian Young, Nina Lalli, Katherine Krause, Jon Natchez, John Fireman, and everyone who helped Launch me. I'd launch you right back.

Thanks to the residents of Rutland Road, and to the astonishing ladies of the book club in particular.

Thanks to Dave Daley, for the honor of being his guinea pig.

Thanks to my agent, Jenni Ferrari-Adler, and her wonderful family, Jofie and Mabel.

Thanks to Stephanie Creaturo, my extremely flexible therapist.

Thanks to Laura and Michael Royal, my wildly supportive in-laws.

Thanks to my family: Susan, Peter, and Ben Straub, who require me to speak in metaphors (see dedication), because I love them too much to say so with a straight face.

And finally: thanks to my husband, Michael Fusco, who would have made this book with a needle and thread if he'd had to. Without you, I'd be sunk.